SAVAGE TRUTH

A HIGH SCHOOL BULLY ROMANCE

HIDDEN VALLEY ELITE SERIES
BOOK TWO

ISLA VAUGHN

ARROWSCOPE PRESS, LLC

Savage Truth

Copyright © 2023 Isla Vaughn

(p) ISBN-13: 978-1-951919-43-6

(e) ISBN-13: 978-1-951919-42-9

Publisher: Arrowscope Press, LLC; www.arrowscopepress.com

Editing— Kate B., Line Editor, Brittany M., Proofreader, Red Adept Editing

Cover Design—T.E. Black Designs; www.teblackdesigns.com

Interior Formatting & Design— Arrowscope Press, LLC; www.arrowscope-press.com

CHAPTER ONE

RILEY

ole Savage is a class-A MVP. A most valuable prick. A blackmailing MVP.

I stormed into the Savages' house, slammed the slider with extra force, flipped the lock, and left the big jerk outside. No one had been there when I met my uncle in the backyard—I'd made sure of it. So how Cole knew I was on the patio was the question. It was as if he had a GPS stuck to my ass.

Of all the guys Mom could date—and I say that liberally because real relationships weren't a thing with our way of life—it had to be Cole's dad. I couldn't wrap my head around it. Hell would freeze over before I would believe that whole thing was legit.

Mom and I ran cons to survive, never hitting the same town twice—except for Santa Monica, California, where Lucas Savage lived. And since Mom had insisted I move into their dumb house with her and her boyfriend, there I was. What should've happened was a con with Lucas as her mark while I extracted pertinent information from his sons, Cole and Damon.

Cole was a nightmare. a drool-worthy fantasy with broad

shoulders, a washboard stomach, and a face that could grace magazines and the big screen. I couldn't stop thinking about him. He was still a pain in my ass.

I grabbed handfuls of my hair and tugged, trying to calm down in their gourmet kitchen, which by itself was bigger than most of the places we'd lived. He made me so mad. No one, and I mean no one, had ever caught Mom or me with my uncle, and there was very important reason for that. Cole had information on me that could be my ultimate downfall—Mom's too.

He has a name. But even uncle Ronan's first name would have been enough for someone to find out who he was. It wouldn't take long to tie Mom and me to him then learn our given last names and where we came from, despite our various aliases muddying the waters.

No matter how hard I tried, I couldn't shake the foreboding sense that even though Mom planned to give us everything we'd never had via her relationship with Lucas, it would inevitably blow up in our faces.

Cole and I played a cat-and-mouse game of blackmail, and for the first time since we'd started, I was worried. But I knew Cole wanted me to be.

I couldn't dwell on what-ifs. I would find a way to turn the tables. I made a detour to the laundry room, where I dumped my warm clothes from the dryer into a laundry basket then took it upstairs to fold and put away. I refused to look out any of the back windows in case Cole was stuck out there. I hoped he was.

I popped my bedroom door open with a hip check and stopped short. "What the hell are you doing in here?"

Cole sprawled across my luxurious queen-sized bed, wearing that wicked smirk that I'd come to associate with him being up to no good. He looked too damn good, and I didn't trust myself with him.

I dropped the basket of clean clothes near my dresser,

staying five feet from the bed and him. If looks could kill, he would have been dead. I crossed my arms over my chest, leaned a hip against the dresser, and waited for him to talk or, even better, leave.

"I'm not going anywhere until we get a few things straight." His green eyes flashed with determination, and a muscle jumped along his strong jaw. "You've got nothing on me, but—"

"Not true." I straightened, my arms dropping to my sides. I resisted forming fists as I attempted to bluff my way out of whatever nightmare he had planned. "I have a video of you participating in an illegal underground fight, which I bet the Hidden Valley Academy—and especially Thane University—would be interested in seeing."

Cole was a senior, like me, and a star tight end on the academy's team, and I knew he had a scholarship to play at Thane. He didn't need the money because his dad was loaded, but I'd overheard him and the other elite assholes talking about needing scholarships. There must have been a reason, and I was pretty sure it was because Cole and his brother, Damon, hated their father.

There was no way they hated him more than I hated mine.

We all had our issues, and the less he knew about me, the better. I just had to keep him unbalanced, which I found rather difficult.

"You've got nothing, Riley. Remember, I was in your room not too long ago when you were sleeping. I hacked your phone and destroyed the video. It's a good thing you sleep like the dead."

"Only sometimes." That had been an alarmingly off night.

"There weren't any traces of it saved elsewhere. Not your computer, not a hidden flash drive."

I narrowed my eyes. He was right, but I had no intention of letting him know that. I'd watched the video several times before he'd gotten to it. He fought with animalistic abandon, each punch calculated and so very powerful. It sent a thrill racing through me. If only we were on the same team, then maybe… *No.* I couldn't let my mind go there. The only team that made sense was Mom, Uncle Ronan, and me. The way it always had been and would be.

He flexed his abs beneath his too-tight T-shirt, distracting me for a moment, then smoothly rolled to his feet. His superior athleticism showed in everything from the cut of his muscles and broad shoulders to his rock-hard chest and tapered waist. I didn't understand how someone well over six feet tall and built like a brick wall could move so quietly. It was disturbing and a little frightening. I raised my chin. I wasn't scared of him.

He was nothing like what Mom and I had dealt with in the past. Cole was child's play, or so I kept reminding myself.

"You better be sure of that because the repercussions of that video…" I left my statement hanging. He was right. I had nothing since he erased it, but I wasn't going to admit that.

"I'm sure." He smirked then advanced. "Soon, I'll know what you're hiding, and then I'll go to Dad, and he'll kick you both out the front door."

Heat flashed, and the gold in his eyes turned molten. "Unless"—his gaze dropped to my lips before meeting my eyes again—"you agree to my terms."

I moved forward, his intoxicating spicy, oceanic scent luring me to touch him. I resisted, but barely. "You don't have anything. So what? I talked with someone I call my uncle. He might be related. He might not be."

"Your mom met with a man the other night. I have a recording of her telling him to wait a little while longer and that she loves him. What do you think my dad will do when he hears that?"

"I hate you." Something dark and dangerous sizzled between us, and I moved out of his reach because if he kissed me, my willpower would snap.

"You'll owe me a weekly favor of my choice."

I curled my upper lip, letting my anger show. He would ask for something sleazy. A thrill raced down my spine, but I hid behind my appalled expression. If he knew I wanted more from him... I couldn't go there. He'd already had the football players freeze me out at school. No one would date me, guys were afraid of me, and the Barbie Club—aka the Bitch Squad or the Elites' Entourage—took turns bullying me. At least that part was amusing.

"Tomorrow is Friday, and I have a game. You can start this weekend by doing my laundry." His sinful lips curled into a wide grin.

That asshole was laughing at me. I narrowed my eyes. But the joke was on him. I'd been doing laundry since I was ten—not that I would admit that to him. "The housekeeper does your laundry." Louisa was more of a mom than a housekeeper, and I doubted she would be okay with me taking over that task.

He sidestepped me on his way to the door. "From now on, you're my maid."

I followed as he passed through my open door. When he turned, it looked like he was going to say something else when he clamped his mouth shut and a wall came down in his eyes, locking me out.

Before slamming my door in his face, I peered down the hallway to see what had caught Cole's attention. Lucas was coming up the stairs. I flashed his dad a fake smile then snagged Cole's focus back to me and whispered, "You can go fuck yourself."

He laughed, and I swear I thought I heard him reply, "Not if I fuck you first."

Unsettled by how much I wanted that, I hurried back into my room and shut my door. I leaned against it, anger at lusting after his body vibrating through me, when I heard his dad stop Cole in the hallway. I pressed my ear to the door.

"I'm glad to see you and Riley getting along, but remember that she's off-limits."

Cole grunted something noncommittal.

"Raelyn and I are trying to make this work, and I need you boys to behave. After the stunt you and your brother pulled with the party, Raelyn was very concerned. Let me make this crystal clear for you and Damon. No sleeping with your soon-to-be stepsister."

"She's not my type."

That fucker. I'll show him how much I'm "not his type." That kiss at the fight the other night told me something very different.

"Good. Tomorrow night, Raelyn and I'll be at the game for the alum introductions. She wants to do dinner out with all of us. You will come to that and behave."

Interesting. I didn't need to hear anything more because I had a very good idea of how to even the playing field. All I had to do was get Cole to hit on me in front of his father. I flopped onto my bed and tried hard not to laugh. I would do his laundry and even clean his room whether he wanted me to or not, wearing my skimpiest shorts and tightest shirts. *Let's see how tall and proud he walks when I put him in his place—which is hands-off of me.*

Entering the Savage house was surreal after school… or any time. I sighed in relief when I found the kitchen empty. Even Louisa wasn't around. I opened the fridge and grabbed an apple, intent on barricading myself in my room for the rest of the night.

I turned and stopped short, unable to prevent a scowl on my face when Lucas appeared in front of me. *Do any of the Savages make a sound?* It was like living with panthers. They would be on me, ready for the kill before I even heard as much as a scuff of their shoes.

"I'm glad you're here, Riley. I've been meaning to talk to you."

It was clear what my mom saw in him. He looked like both Cole and Damon, just older. That didn't mean I trusted him or wanted to be there. I didn't say a word. I just waited to hear what asinine thing Cole had managed to pin on me again.

"Your mom and I talked, and she swears that you were not the one to throw the party. In that moment, I was shocked by the mess and not thinking clearly." He grimaced. "Which one of my sons threw the party?"

Silence was best, so I continued to stare at him. I was no rat.

His lips twitched like he was suppressing a smile. "I see."

I doubted that very much. I took a bite of the apple without breaking eye contact, preferring to know where he was at all times. I didn't get any creepy vibes from him, but I didn't like him either.

"We got off on the wrong foot, but I want you to know that I love your mom very much, and I will do everything in my power to keep her safe."

That was where our opinion differed. "It won't be enough, and we won't be staying. And as for loving Mom"—I shrugged— "you say that, but you're getting the good side of her right now. You haven't known each other long enough to wade through the bad. And when that happens, no infatuation will be enough to protect any of us."

"Your mom is the only woman I've ever loved."

That shocked me. "What about Cole and Damon's mom? Or were you too busy cheating on her with whoever your new infatuation was?" Low blow, and I was sure Mom would be horrified since she was so into this guy, but his comment made me sick. No matter how much of a jerk Cole was, it was a good thing he wasn't here to listen to this.

"It's complicated. I cared deeply for her, but it's not the same as what I've always felt for your mom." His pained expression cleared, and determination flared in his blue eyes, which were so like Damon's. "This is our time, and I won't let anything— especially something from your past—stand in our way."

Oh wow, she told him stuff? That comment was barely veiled. We never told anyone anything. It made me wonder what else I didn't know about their relationship. And gross. I didn't want to go there.

"And this goes without saying, but I'll ensure you're safe too."

I huffed. There was no way he could stop or even slow down what would come for us. And there was no point in trying to convince him otherwise. We would leave in the dead of night, like always.

I had nothing more to say and clamped my lips together, gripping the apple in my right hand. He took the cue and left. Alone in the kitchen, I couldn't stop tremors from running through me as I considered the disaster Mom had landed us in. Needing even a small release, I flipped Lucas's retreating form off with my left hand and an emphatic "fuck you" under my breath.

"That was interesting."

I whirled around in the direction of the deep voice and launched the apple I held with everything I had. My heart thundered in fear, and I shifted to the balls of my feet, ready to run.

Damon stood in the open pantry, his fist wrapped around the apple that would have hit him in the middle of the chest.

I gulped air, and adrenaline coursed through me as I fought the urge to run.

"Nice aim."

"How long have you been here?" Not that it mattered to me, but it wouldn't help the rocky relationship between the men in this house if he'd heard too much.

"Since you got this apple from the fridge." His face darkened, and I recognized what his opponents must have seen on the football field or in the ring. "Interesting. I'm glad I stayed in there. You learn something new every day."

Whatever that meant didn't matter. Nothing would change. "Well, it's been real, Demon." I purposely used his nickname as I backed away, making a beeline for the stairs.

A part of me wondered what would have happened if it had been Cole instead. I doubted it would have made a difference, but there were some clues in what Lucas said about my past that I didn't need Cole learning. *Will Damon tell him?*

A roar rippled through the crowd, gaining in strength as Cass and I weaved our way through the nearly full bleachers to the empty seats we'd spotted. She'd convinced me to come to the game, which hadn't been difficult. Mom and Lucas were here too. She'd said Lucas and some other alumni were being recognized at halftime. Supposedly, it was a big deal. Guess he was good back in the day, not that I cared even a little.

The team took the field, and I glanced at the players, searching for Cole, who wasn't hard to find. I knew the way he moved. My stomach clenched. I cursed the way my body reacted to him. Insane. No one had ever caused me to respond even a fraction as much as he did from a single glance.

The excitement from the crowd was infectious, and I leaned forward in anticipation. Cass nudged my shoulder with hers.

"Wait until you see them. It's an experience."

"How are they different than any other high school team?"

Cass grinned then tucked her dark hair behind her ears. She had a chic look that not many could pull off. "Cole's projected to go into the NFL from Thane."

I scrunched my nose. *Seriously?* "How can they know that about a high schooler?"

She laughed. "Just watch him on the field. Phoenix too. He's the QB. Even though he's a year younger, scouts have been watching him since freshman year when he made varsity."

"A family of NFLers? That's a thing?"

Cass shrugged, the corners of her mouth twitching. "Okay, Miss My-Dives-Rival-Olympians."

I rolled my eyes. "Not likely. But back to them…"

"Here's the history." She leaned in and lowered her voice. "Cole's dad is rumored to have been chosen for the draft. I guess he was high up in whatever it is… picks?" She waved her hand. "Not sure what that's called, but his stats were good enough to give him a ranking that said he'd go in the first few rounds. Then he… dropped out."

"Of college?" I'd never paid attention to professional sports outside of diving.

"No, from the draft. No idea what happened, but that's what my dad told me, and he's a sports fanatic."

"Okay, so maybe that explains Cole, but Phoenix too?"

"Damon and Shane are also exceptional players, but Cole and Phoenix are able to do things that my dad says are legendary. And Shane and Phoenix's dad is in the NFL."

"So he taught them?" It would have made sense and would have given them a leg up.

"No. I don't think he's a part of their lives. But talent is all up in their blood. My dad can't shut up about it after he watches one of their games, which he does religiously. He's "—she searched the crowd then pointed to a center area near the top of the bleachers—"he and Mom are there, decked out in gold and black."

That didn't narrow it down at all, as those were our school colors. I nodded, going with it. "If he's so great, will the NFL draft him after he graduates this year?"

Cass shrugged. "I don't know anything about that. But I heard he's going to Thane University."

It was a Division 1 school and where I would apply if I actually went away to college, which I doubted. But their diving team tempted me to drink the Kool-Aid. "What about you?"

"I'm going there too." Her gaze shifted to the front of the bleachers where Piper and her squad were doing some cheers. "Piper is too. Despite how stupid she is when it comes to Cole, she's really smart."

I thought a moment and decided it didn't bother me. "How did you find that out? About Piper, I mean."

"I'm friends with Brooke, who's tight with Piper, remember?"

"Oh, yeah."

"That's where you'll go, right? The diving team is outstanding. I don't think you could pass it up if you got offered a spot on their team. Would it bother you that Piper will be there?" Cass shifted so she could look at my face.

"No." I shrugged. "She doesn't upset me." I cast another glance at the blond Barbie going through her cheer routine. It did bother me a little that she wasn't over Cole. I wasn't sure she ever would be. She had it bad for him, which was why she acted the way she did. Given Cole's ever-changing emotions, though, most of the school didn't freeze me out as much anymore. They pretty much ignored me in the halls. Including Piper.

"She never meant anything to Cole." Cass's penetrating look was all-knowing.

"I know." My voice was subdued. A part of me felt bad for Piper. But she wasn't my problem, and Cole didn't give her the time of day anymore. Putting all thoughts of her from my mind, I shifted my gaze to the field, where the players lined up.

The center snapped the ball, and I found myself leaning forward. Some of the players ran routes, and the other team covered them as Phoenix found his target. Then he launched the ball in what even I would call a beautiful pass to Cole, who plucked it out of the air. Damon blocked another player and cleared a space for Cole, who took off down the field. Holy crap was he fast!

My heart pounded, and I leapt to my feet with the rest of the academy's fans as he crossed into the endzone. Even I knew a touchdown on the first play was something to shout about. The minutes flew by, and Cass laughed at me when my jaw almost came unhinged at another shockingly good play. They made the other team look like fools. It was crazy.

I finally understood why the Elites were treated the way they were. On the field, they were legends. It was that simple. And while I was shocked and seriously impressed, I wondered if I could shake things up if we ran into each other at halftime. A small grin curved my lips. I had to try.

CHAPTER TWO

COLE

I lived and breathed the game—the hard hits, running down the field to catch one of Phoenix's perfect throws, the grass, the strategy, every goddammed bit of it. We were in the last stretch, and Shane lined up in such a way that the other team shifted to provide heavy coverage at the line. That left me.

Damon shuffled his feet, ready to block. The crowd was ballistic. It was impossible to hear my teammates.

Dad was in the stands. The school planned to honor some of the alumni at halftime, and he was one of them. I didn't care about that. What I did care about was that Thane's recruiter was there.

In the back of my mind, I wondered if Riley was, too, and if so, what she thought. Some part of me wanted her to watch me play.

Phoenix stomped his foot, and the center hiked the ball. I took off at a sprint. There was no looking back. My cleats dug into the ground as I wove through the secondary, keeping their cornerback just out of reach. A thud to my right meant that Damon had taken out that fast safety, keeping the path clear. I took two more long strides, hooked to the right, and looked up. The ball soared overhead. I stretched a hand high, catching it with the tips of my fingers, then pulled it into my chest and put on a burst of speed.

Damon kept pace beside me, barreling into another player who hit the ground. With three more strides, and I crossed the goal line. The crowd was on their feet as our kicker set up for the extra point. The safety hiked it, Phoenix held it, and the kicker's foot connected. It sailed between the posts.

We had several minutes left in the second quarter, and I hustled off the field, making way for the defensive line. It wasn't long until we were back out there, our defense having kept the other team to three and out. I focused only on my teammates, the opponents, and what play our QB called. Nothing else mattered.

One day, this game will be my career.

Phoenix threw for sixty yards in the last few minutes of the half, which culminated in a perfect pass to Shane for the final touchdown before halftime.

Still pumped, I came off the field and headed to the locker room. Piper appeared after I took a few steps down the hall. She moved in front, blocking me, and my impatience spiked. Not only did I have to deal with her—and it wasn't the best time— but I thought I glimpsed Riley, the only girl who occupied my mind of late.

In her cheer uniform, Piper looked like someone else's wet dream. I could recognize how beautiful she was, but there was no spark between us. Maybe there had been at one time, but it was long since dead. She stepped close and put her hands on my chest.

"Back off, Piper. You have no claim to me."

Tears misted over her big blue eyes as my teammates parted around us, continuing to the locker room. "But I love you." Her lower lip quivered. "It's you and me and always has been."

I got what she was saying—she was the girl I hooked up with. It was casual, and I knew she wasn't sleeping around. It made things easy, but I couldn't do that anymore. Obviously, she'd caught feelings, but there would never be anything there for me.

"Think, Piper. You like being seen with me, and sometimes I like fucking you. But there is no relationship. I made that very clear. And to put something else out there, I don't plan on getting married. So don't get any ideas." She used to talk about it. I knew it was her long-term plan. "At all. As in never. I'm not interested, so back the hell off with the bullshit possessiveness." I shifted, forcing her hands to fall away. "Go back before you get in trouble for stepping out at halftime."

Cheerleading didn't matter to me, but I knew it did to her. With each step away from her, I scanned every face, searching for Riley. I swore I'd seen her. *There.* I found her not far from the entrance, her warm brown eyes glittering with a challenge.

I sensed rather than saw Piper behind me, watching everything play out. I didn't like how cruel she and the other girls were to Riley, even though I'd inspired it. That was my role alone.

When Eliana Defrieze slipped into an open space on my right, I realized the timing couldn't be more perfect both to discourage Piper and to take the heat off Riley.

"Hey, Cole. Are you coming to my party tonight? It won't be as good as the last one you threw, but"—her tongue slid along her bottom lip as she fixated on mine—"maybe we can find a quiet place and get to know each other better."

I'd known Eliana since second grade when she moved to town. I caught Riley's eye, holding it as I leaned down and brushed a kiss across Eliana's mouth. "Sounds good. I'll see you there."

One of the last to enter the locker room for halftime, I walked past Riley without even looking at her. Her presence stuck in my mind, taking up entirely too much space. *Why is she here?* I joined the guys as the coach went over what he expected for the next half, but my head wasn't in the game.

Halftime was short. We came out to catch the tail end of the show. Dad was walking off the field with the other old-timers who got to relive their glory days with the ceremony. I grunted at Dad's slap to the back.

"Great game. Let's see some more of it."

Then he was gone, and I attempted to tuck away how different his demeanor was from the other men who came off the field. I hated to say it, but he had the same driven expression that I felt inside me with each play, and Mom's comment from last year resurfaced, throwing me off balance even more than Riley had. *"You know your father was invited to the draft. He had several teams talking to him and would have played in the NFL if he hadn't changed his mind at the last minute and chosen to open a law firm after college."*

Something wasn't sitting right.

"Cole!"

Coach's shout snapped me out of it, and I took the field with the rest of the team, thinking that I'd refocused. But I hadn't. As much as I tried to keep my head in the game, I was off. I over or underran passes, missed blocks, and fumbled in the red zone, so Coach benched me. It was all Riley's fucking fault. Damon went in to save the lead I almost single-handedly gave away.

After the win, the locker room was loud, and everyone except my brother and cousins gave me a wide berth. Phoenix put his helmet in the locker next to mine then sat to remove his cleats. It was coming. I didn't even try to stop him.

"What the fuck was that?"

I curled my hand into a fist and forced myself to relax. It wasn't his fault that Riley was in my head or that her being there near the locker room at halftime had flipped some switch in my mind, taking me from driven and focused on the game to reliving everything about how she felt and tasted. It wasn't his problem that I wanted to get her under me at all costs. I was fucking obsessed with her, and it needed to stop before the price was my future. "Riley was here earlier."

Phoenix stared then blinked. I'd succeeded in shocking him too.

"Yeah, I don't even know how to process this shit."

"You're turning into Shane." His words were cold and harsh.

A wave of anger rushed through me, but I held back. He was right, after all. Shane was so whipped that he didn't even realize that Tracey wanted his potential career more than she wanted him.

"You're going to throw everything away for a piece of ass. Just like my brother." Phoenix stood inches from my face. Fury crackled between us. "Get her out of your system. It doesn't matter how. Fuck her or someone else. Whatever it takes. Because if you don't, that scout here earlier won't bother coming back."

Damon dropped down on the bench, and not even a second later, Shane did too. The other players drifted to the showers or were dressing to leave. We kept our voices low. This wasn't anyone's business.

"This about Riley?"

I leveled my brother with a look that would have made anyone else run for cover. "What if it is?"

"You need to figure out how to let it go. You want to take it out on her mom? Go for it. But Riley isn't that bad."

"What's changed that's got you on her team?" It bothered me, but not nearly as much as I thought it would.

Damon shrugged before getting to his feet. "She didn't rat us out about the party."

"So?" Dad already knew we were behind it.

"I'm just saying. She's not that bad, and she doesn't like our dad." He winked before heading out. "Something to think about," he said over his shoulder.

As if I could get her out of my head as it was.

"I'm with Damon on this one, cuz." Shane got up and followed my brother.

"His opinion in this doesn't matter." Phoenix snorted then slapped me on the shoulder. "Look, dude, Damon has a point about Riley not being what you think she is. But none of that matters. What does is how you'll handle the next game. You can't afford to fuck up again. Get things figured out with her before next week."

"I will." *Eliana could be a distraction.* Something told me that if I hooked up with Riley, one time would never be enough. I would let my dad think his word was law. It wasn't. The decision was mine. "Are you going to Eliana's party tonight?"

"Yeah." Phoenix closed his locker. "I'll see you there."

I finished grabbing my stuff and followed him, only to find my dad and Raelyn waiting for me in the hall. *Fuck.* I refused to look at her. When I did, all I could see was Mom lying on her bed, surrounded by empty pill bottles, her sightless eyes stuck open.

"What happened in the last half?"

Dad's frown caused mine to deepen. "Don't know. What?" I stepped closer, unable to stop myself. The inner conflict surrounding all things Riley was mind-fucking me. "You've never had an off game?"

"On that last pass, you looked behind you instead of up. Rookie mistake and far beneath you." Dad rose an eyebrow. Raelyn remained frozen by his side. "I saw Thane's scout here tonight. Whoever's on your mind, it isn't the time."

"I'm well aware of what's at stake." We were locked in a stare, and I refused to be the one to break it.

"Why don't we head home?" Raelyn's voice drew Dad's gaze.

"We can get ready to go out to eat and drive in one car from there."

I didn't bother responding. I turned and headed toward my car, ignoring Dad saying my name in warning. *We're going out to eat tonight? Fine. Whatever. Wonder how well that'll go with Riley there.*

The drive home was an autopiloted blur. Dad had been on my case lately. I only had this year, and I would be out from under his roof—and if the scholarship held, his thumb, at least for the most part. The trust didn't turn over to me until I was twenty-one, but I did have some money saved from the fights. It would be enough for whatever I needed.

I threw the car into park, shut off the engine, then went inside and took the stairs two at a time. At the open door to my room, I dropped my bag on the floor. Everything in me froze in shock when I saw Riley lying on my bed. I took in her toned legs, crossed at the ankles, all the way to her tiny little shorts. I had to fight from lunging forward and climbing on top of her. She looked like heaven with her long hair fanned out on my pillow and her breasts pushing against a form-fitting, washed-out-navy T-shirt. A slow, sexy grin curved her plump lips, and I continued to imagine everything I wanted to do to them.

"It's good that baby bro doesn't go soft when the chips are down."

What the hell? I narrowed my eyes, not liking the innuendo or how hypersexual she was. "You came to watch me. And I'm more than willing to show you how there's nothing soft about me." The room seemed to shrink. All I could see was Riley, and she was messing with my head. "But you'll have to wait for that. I'm going to a party tonight. You have grass stains to get out of my uniform."

Her lips turned down in the sexiest pout I'd ever seen. Then she rolled off my bed, and I locked onto the gentle sway of her hips. Sweet fuck, she made me so hard.

"I'll get right on that." She rested a hand on my chest then turned away, far too close, on her way to the door.

Her hip brushed against my dick as it strained to get to her. I didn't know what game she played, but I didn't like it. Or maybe I liked it too much, which made it much worse.

CHAPTER THREE

RILEY

ole's feet pounded down the stairs, and I sprang into action, hitting the button to connect me to Cassie. With the phone pressed to my ear, I paced my room, willing her to answer. The blinds were down, and I double-checked that the lock was engaged on my door. Two more rings, and she picked up. I flopped onto my bed, so grateful for the lifeline of my first and only friend.

"Hey, Cass. You busy?"

"If you mean busy by hanging with my sister so my parents can go out? Then yeah, my life is golden."

I snorted a laugh. "Ah, sibling problems. I wouldn't understand."

"Stop rubbing it in. One sec. Let me start a movie for her, and then I can talk 'cause I hear the stress in your voice, girl."

While waiting, I put in my earbuds so I could move around without being tied to holding the phone then turned onto my back to stare at the ceiling with—I-shit-you-not— a chandelier. In my seventeen years, I'd never had a room as fancy as this one. I'd never lived in a McMansion, either, and I wouldn't get used to it. Anything could happen and force Mom and me to pack up and leave. I couldn't get too comfortable.

"Okay, I'm back. Sara's even got snacks and a drink. There shouldn't be any interruptions for at least an hour. So what's up?"

I filled her in on everything, including how Cole found the video I'd taken of the fight on my phone and deleted it and what I overheard his dad say in the hallway.

"So let me get this straight," Cass said. "Cole's dad has forbidden him from making a move on you?"

"Yep."

"And you were in his room tonight when he got home from the game in very short shorts and a tight tee?"

"Correct."

"What's the plan here? Are you seriously going to do his laundry? I'm down for the teasing part because I know where you're going with that. He kisses you again—"

"Not a hardship."

"Exactly. But it's payback time if he does it in front of his father." She laughed under her breath. "I love it. When and how will this go down?"

"We're supposed to go out to dinner in about five minutes. I need to change. Cole was already downstairs. I'm not sure where Damon is or if they'll even go."

"Somehow, I doubt it. There's a party tonight at Eliana's."

"Who's she? And do I need to worry about her too? I already have the Barbie Club on my back."

"Not important. If anything, she's a drive-by for him. Let's focus on what you're going to do at the dinner. That would be a great time to get him to kiss you."

"I'm not sure if that'll work because he'll be on guard. But it's perfect for making him as hot and bothered as I can."

"Wear your hair up. And definitely sit next to him. If you can accidentally brush against him, do that."

I laughed. "It's like you've done this before." So had I— about five minutes before, in his room.

"Matt's not a fast mover. I do what I must to encourage him. I think he's still a little wary because of seeing me with Damon that one time."

I chuckled. "One time seems to be too many with the boys in this school."

"You're talking about the wimps we have on the football team?"

"Nailed it."

She had tried to introduce me to one of the guys that had shown interest, but Cole had gotten to what seemed like every guy. They were terrified of being seen talking to me, which meant no dating for me. It wasn't unusual, given how much I'd moved around, and I could deal with it. But it would have been great to take my mind off Cole. He took up entirely too much real estate inside my head.

"Okay, I'll do that at dinner. But I'll have better luck with him kissing me again if we're in the kitchen or downstairs... where I hope his father is too."

"Then that's your goal. What are you gonna do about stupid maid duty?"

I shrugged. "I'm good with it. I can search his room. Laundry isn't a big deal to me. And if a red shirt finds its way into a load of whites..."

Cassie laughed. "I love it!"

"Hey, I've been meaning to ask you why you're friends with me when everyone else is scared of the Elites?" I'd thought it strange from the start and knew she was friendly with one of the Barbie Squad but not much else. There was a beat of silence, and I worried that I'd crossed some sort of line before her sigh traveled through the connection.

"I've known Brooke all my life. We used to do ballet at the

same studio, but in junior high, things got hard for her. We were close—more than she is with the popular crowd."

"I haven't seen you guys talk to each other."

"Nope. And we won't. Being in the top tier is everything to her, and she won't do anything to rock that boat. Let's just say I have some information on her that she doesn't want known around school."

I stretched out on my bed, crossing my legs at my ankles. "What kind of information?"

"You can't use this against her. Things would go bad—for her, anyway. And even though we aren't close anymore, I don't want to cause her pain."

The seedy underbelly of being popular. I could guess, but I would rather have had confirmation about why Brooke kept Cassie protected from the other girls' wrath. "Okay. I promise not to breathe a word about it."

"Ballet is a big thing to Brooke. I think she wants to dance in New York for one of the companies out there after high school. Anyway, she was a little chubby in junior high, and our instructor was hard on her, pushing her to lose weight, eat better—"

"Or not at all?" Anger climbed my spine. I didn't have to like her to hate how she was treated.

"Yeah, pretty much. I found her in the bathroom more than one time, puking. She had an issue with bulimia. Then there was the cutting. Only in places that wouldn't show. But I saw one day. She swore me to secrecy, and I only agreed if she stopped."

"Did she?"

"I think so. I made sure to go to the beach with her as often as possible and get in the water. I figured the salt water would be a little bit of a deterrent. But she also had a growth spurt, and all the softer spots that our instructor was hard on her about melted away."

"That sucks." Completely ridiculous. But I could also understand Brooke and Cassie's positions better with that information. "I swear I won't say a word. Thanks for sharing that with me."

"Well, it hasn't been easy for you at school."

"It's not that bad." I suddenly had some respect for Brooke. She had never openly picked on me. Not that it bothered me that the others did, but it showed what type of person she was.

"Back to Cole. I don't get it."

"Don't get what?"

"So what if Cole found the video? There's another fight tonight. Record another one."

I felt nauseous just thinking about it. "It's not worth the trouble. And I have an aversion to cops. And they would be involved if I leaked the video. There are other things I can do to get to him."

"Really?" Disbelief and sarcasm were heavy in that single word. "There's more to it than that."

"No." Beads of sweat broke out along my hairline. She was too close to the truth, something I didn't even want to admit to myself. Because it couldn't be true that there was more to my feelings for Cole other than lust. I didn't do that—ever. If Mom and Uncle Ronan had taught me anything, it was to keep myself physically and emotionally guarded around others.

"You know I don't believe you."

I pushed out a breath, rolling onto my stomach and bunching some of the duvet under my arms like a pillow. "Believe it. If I post it, he could face jail time. He's eighteen, and I bet some of the kids he fights are underage."

"Oh," Cass whispered. "I didn't think of it that way. Legal charges would be serious and something that their dad may not be able to get them out of."

"Right. It's more for me to torture him with and hold over his head. But I don't want to take things too far. Plus, it would give his brother and cousins ammunition. If I did something like that, they would come at me full force, adding to whatever Cole could do before being hauled away to jail." I shuddered at the thought of cops. No way would I do that. I wouldn't want to be in that position, and some of them could be influenced by who we were running from.

"Fair point. But I still call bullshit on the real reason why you won't do it. You like him. You *really* like him."

I snorted. "What's not to like… physically? It's the rest that I'm not into."

"Keep telling yourself that, Riles." She laughed. "Have fun torturing Cole."

"You know I will." I joined in the laughter. It was more fun than I'd thought it would be. "I've got to run, but are you doing anything with Matt this weekend?"

"Tomorrow morning, but that's it so far. Want to get lunch or go to the cove?"

"Yes. Let me get back to you on where and when."

Mom yelled up the stairs.

"My mom's calling. Gotta go to dinner. And Cass…"

"Yeah?"

"Thanks."

"Always. Make him your bitch."

My laugh sounded devious even to me. I planned to do that and more. I couldn't wait for Cole to break down and kiss me again, no matter the consequences.

"The last time I saw you was when you were a tiny little thing, just learning to walk. And now, I can't believe you look so much like your mom did when she was about your age."

I choked on the steak I was trying to swallow, trying hard not to throw it back up. My fork clattered to the plate, garnering the attention of the couple seated at the table to our left. *Please don't say where that was.* Cole didn't need any more information on us.

I remained silent. I had no reply to Lucas's comment. Thankfully, I didn't need one.

"Nice, Dad." Damon's voice was devoid of emotion as he drew everyone's attention. "What's next? Are you going to tell us that she's our long-lost sister? That you're really her father?"

Mom's wide eyes caught and held mine. "No, Damon," she answered, never breaking eye contact with me. "Lucas is *not* Riley's father."

"But you're the other woman. And from what father of the year just admitted, you have been for a long time. Among others. Isn't that right, Dad?" Cole spoke to his dad, but his focus was still on me.

It was entirely too much attention.

"I know you're still angry with me, both of you. But this isn't the time," Lucas said regretfully, looking away.

I kept my gaze fixed on Mom. I could read the sorrow that pulled at the corners of her eyes. It would have been much easier for her if I had been his daughter. My father was a monster, and if we weren't careful, he would find and kill us.

I suppressed a shudder, but not well enough. I felt Cole's eyes burning a hole into the side of my face. Then his large hand rested on the top of my thigh, momentarily stopping my heart and freezing time. As if he had some magical pull, I turned my head, catching his smoldering green eyes with my stricken ones. I didn't want him to see the terror inside me and shut down all emotion, shoving everything deep inside, where it couldn't give him ammunition to hurt me.

He pressed his lips into a tight line as Damon continued to harass their dad. I wasn't listening. I couldn't hear anything when Cole looked at me like he would slay all my dragons. If only it were true and hatred didn't exist between us.

But it did. And I had to remember that.

"Riley." Mom's voice helped to break whatever spell Cole had over me.

I focused on her. "Yeah?"

"I asked if you wanted dessert."

Her smile was strained. Lucas and Damon were glaring at each other, and Cole was still focused on me. The heavy weight of his hand acted to ground me enough that I could break free from the past that Lucas had so casually brought up. "No. I'm full. Are we ready to go?" *Please let us leave this trainwreck of a dinner.*

It wasn't long before we left. Nothing good would have come of staying. Cole and Damon had driven to the restaurant in a separate car, but I'd unfortunately gone with the adults. No one said anything as we piled into our respective vehicles. My phone buzzed in my pocket, and I slipped it out as I climbed into the back of Lucas's SUV. Cassie had texted to tell me there was another fight tonight. She couldn't go but wanted to pass along the information in case I wanted to. I didn't. Dinner had been draining, and I was still trying to figure out the dynamic between Mom and Lucas.

Since the address she'd sent wasn't the old fieldhouse, I figured it would be safe to sneak into school and use the pool, as it was too late to dive safely at the cove. I just needed to wait long enough for everyone to settle their plans.

Once we were back at the house, minus Cole and Damon, I sat in one of the window seats with a book I'd found in their library. There was a section of romance novels that must have been their mom's. She seemed to have enjoyed office romance. It wasn't really my thing, but it was better than any of the lawyer textbooks and science fiction that I'd found.

Reading *Falling for the Boss* would do while I waited for Cole's laundry to finish in the dryer. I couldn't believe I was doing it. But if he returned unexpectedly and caught me in his room, it was a good enough reason for me to be there. Another advantage would be Lucas seeing me with Cole's laundry. I had plans for that too.

And I would follow through because of that comment about the grass stains on his uniform. He'd meant to put me in my place. Even though I could make him hard, I was beneath him— a grifter.

It was late, but I wasn't tired. Cole and Damon were at their stupid underground fight. Lucas was watching a movie with Mom, and with them was the last place I wanted to be. I could hear them laughing and peeked in a couple of times. They hadn't caught me, which was the point. Mom was snuggled against his side, wearing leggings, a T-shirt, and all her makeup scrubbed off her face. It was the most natural I'd seen her around anyone other than Uncle Ronan or me.

I had a bad feeling in the pit of my stomach about it all. I'd never seen her so happy. And as much as I wanted to hate Lucas, I couldn't because of how Mom was around him. But even if I did feel a tiny sliver of gratitude toward Lucas for making her happy, that in no way meant I would go easy on Cole.

I needed to get out of there. A soft *ding* sounded, and I took that as my cue to grab Cole's laundry from the dryer and take it up to his room. I drew the line at folding it. I flung it onto his bed and began systematically searching for the key I knew he had to the school. It didn't take long. He'd left one on his dresser, and it had to be the one. There weren't any others.

On my way out, I stopped short as Mom breezed into the kitchen, carrying two empty wineglasses.

She stopped when she saw the bag slung over my shoulder, and her eyebrows climbed her forehead. "You're diving? It's dark out."

"I can sneak into the school."

She nodded. That was the thing about us—we didn't play by the rules, so my breaking into the school didn't faze her. But it seemed something had as she turned to face me with the weight of her stare.

"I don't know what's going on between you and Lucas's boys, but please, Riles, it's not just me who needs this. We both do."

What about what I need? I didn't voice it, but I wish she would've asked. Because living there wasn't what I'd wanted to happen. *How does she not see the writing on the wall?* Cole may have wanted me, but he also hated me or what I represented. And when he found out about our past, and Lucas did too— because I highly doubted that Mom had told him everything— would we escape in time? Somehow, I wasn't so sure.

I didn't respond but grabbed my bag and slammed out of the house. I expected her to follow, but by the time I got my car started and backed down the driveway, it was clear that I was wrong. It wasn't the first time she'd chosen Lucas over me, and I suspected it wouldn't be the last.

When I got to school, it was late, and I knew it would be empty except for the janitorial staff. I just had to avoid them, which wasn't difficult. I parked by the entrance closest to the pool. The lighting was dim around the building. I swept the area, checking for hidden threats because it was never a good idea to expect someplace to be safe. Dad's goons could be anywhere, according to Uncle Ronan. He and Mom had taught me to be aware at all times, and it stuck. Even though she thought this was a haven for us, I had a hard time believing it and knew a part of her was skeptical, too, because I'd caught her scanning the restaurant parking lot.

I tried the key in the lock, and a sense of victory flooded me when it turned. I grinned at the prospect of keeping the key for myself. I could hide it somewhere in the house. He'd expect to find it in my room, where it would not be.

In the locker room, I shed my clothes and shoved them into my bag before pulling out my towel and taking everything into the pool area. I'd put my bathing suit on under my clothes, not wanting to deal with changing.

The humidity was a balm to my stressed-out senses. I dropped my bag then went immediately to the high-dive ladder. The rungs dug into my bare feet. I hadn't bothered to do anything with my hair, and it hung down my back. No one was there to reprimand me.

I toed the edge of the board, letting the stillness of the space envelop me as I pictured the dive in my mind, mapping each twist and turn. I pushed off the board and savored that brief pause in the air where I floated for a tiny second before gravity took over. I moved my body through the twists and turns, in complete control, then straightened so that I was a strong line from pointed toes to fingertips as I pierced the water, finding another haven below the surface. I couldn't get enough. I dove deep, enjoying the solitude.

When my lungs screamed for air, I kicked for the surface then swam to the side. Hauling myself out of the pool, I salivated for more. Diving was addictive. It saved me from the stress of life, of constantly moving and changing our appearances, providing an escape from the danger that surrounded us.

A door slammed, and I held my breath, darting my gaze to every hidden corner. It sounded close. I sprang into motion, moving for my bag on the slippery floor.

"I saw your dive."

Shit. The diving coach. I looked over my shoulder, and recognition trickled in, slowly taking the edge off the adrenaline rush but leaving a tingling sensation in my fingertips. *This isn't good. He could get me suspended for being here after hours and without permission or a coach present.*

"I'm not going to ask how you got in here," Coach Thompson said. "After that dive, I expect you here tomorrow at six a.m. for practice. This is your one exception." He started to turn away then clearly thought better of it. "And don't let me catch you here after hours again."

"Yes, sir." I threw on the sweatshirt I'd brought, shoved my feet into my shoes, then raced out the door.

He wants me on the team. A secret part of me was thrilled. I'd never joined one before. It wasn't possible. I paused at my car, but Mom said I could join this time. I got behind the wheel, started the engine, then pulled out of the lot, deciding to commit for the first time to something I wanted more than my next breath.

I'm going to do it.

CHAPTER FOUR

COLE

Water beat down on me, washing the blood away. A light-pink swirl went down the drain. That fight had been a tough one. My body ached, and I couldn't wait to fall into bed. Screw the party. I wasn't in the mood to hook up with Eliana when all I could think about was how Riley was probably asleep in the room across the hall from mine.

My neck cracked when I turned my head, easing a sharp pain into a dull ache. I wasn't sure if it was from the football game or the fight. I'd taken a beating but given one, too, and won. The bruises on my chin, chest, and shin were all worth it. I was sitting at eleven to one. Undefeated would have been better, but I'd take it.

Steam billowed from the shower, fogging the mirror. I stepped out and grabbed my towel from the warming rack. After a quick rubdown to get the excess water off, I wrapped the towel around my waist and walked into my room.

Riley? Exhausted, I had to blink a few times to make sure what I saw was real. Yep, Riley was lying on my bed, looking like a wet dream. That was a horrible idea.

I could hear Dad and Damon talking in the hall. It wasn't

likely that my dad would come up here, but if he did… it could cost me more than I was willing to give. Because of that botched game the other day, which he couldn't stop rehashing, I felt the noose around my neck with the possible loss of my scholarship —I hadn't signed anything yet. Everything was up in the air. If that went away and he refused to pay for college, my chances of being drafted into the NFL would drop.

She crossed one leg over the other at the ankles on my bed, and it was all I could do to remain where I was and not fall on her. Goddammit, I wanted her to stay like I needed my next breath. I needed to stop thinking with my dick. "You need to get out."

She rolled to her knees, a sexy little smirk curving her mouth, and reached for the towel. "You should climb into bed with me."

Blood roared through my body with the graze of her fingers over my chest, and I moved to my door and kicked it shut. Then I turned to her and closed the distance between us, stopping mere inches from kissing her. "This is a bad look on you, all this desperation." Total bullshit. She was beautiful, soft, and so sexy. The desperation was all me.

"I'm not the one looking desperate right now." She pursed her lips and looked pointedly to where my dick was straining against the towel.

"Listen, Baby Girl." She was off-limits, and it was driving me crazy. "You're nothing but a prick tease." I wanted to goad her into letting me have another taste.

Her warm brown eyes darkened, and the air charged between us. All I had to do was push her a little more… "Let me give you some examples: in my room—twice now. After the game. At the restaurant—"

"You're a prick. And I'm not teasing." She rose a perfectly sculpted eyebrow. "All you have to do is ask."

Fuck. There had to have been a reason why I couldn't control myself around her, why I wanted her more than I'd ever wanted anyone.

She got off the bed and stood before me. Then her hand was on my chest—so softly. Her fingers shook as if she'd never touched a man before. *Oh God, she's touching me like she's a fucking virgin.*

My body tensed, and I didn't move an inch for fear of scaring her away. Everywhere her fingers grazed, I felt a zap of electricity. My pulse kicked up another notch. There was something addictive, impossible to resist about her. I'd been with a lot of girls, but none had affected me as she did. I let her skim her fingertips over my abs and up my chest then curl around my shoulders. She was on her toes with her head tilted at just the right angle.

Jesus, my dad was going to kill me. Didn't matter. From the moment she ran into me at school, I'd wanted her. I moved closer then brushed her long chestnut hair over her shoulder to gain access to her neck. I grazed my lips along the slender curve, breathing in her unique scent.

My thumb caressed the sensitive skin where her pulse thundered at the base of her neck. I eased back enough to read her. When her eyes softened and her lips parted, I couldn't resist the pull. Desire charged the connection between us, and it felt right.

I slipped my hand behind her neck to bury my fingers in her hair, moving slowly to give her a choice to pull back. I was tense with the anticipation of kissing her again. I'd dreamed of how she felt, waking drenched in sweat multiple times.

She was so soft. Intoxicating. I brushed my lips against hers, teasing, needing her to move with me. When her tongue darted out to meet mine, my body ignited. Something roared inside me, a deep possessiveness I couldn't deny. Everything in me snapped to attention. The need was primal, stamped into my DNA. I wanted to be her first, her last, and everything in between—which was not normal for me.

Ruthlessly, I shoved the thoughts aside. I would examine them more closely another day.

Her arms wound around my neck, and she buried her fingers in my damp hair, tugging on the strands as her hips pressed into mine. I lifted her into my arms, and she wrapped her legs around my waist.

When she moaned, I deepened the kiss, losing myself in how right it felt to hold her. She was so addictive. Jolts of intense awareness traveled through me, making it harder to stop. I'd never forgotten that first kiss, and I never stopped wanting another. And holy shit, could she kiss.

CHAPTER FIVE

RILEY

I have craved this kiss ever since the first time our lips met last summer.

It measured up to the memory and to my dreams. Different but just as addictive. Everything between us faded: the hate, the games, the distrust. As his lips masterfully moved over mine, that moment was all that mattered.

My head spun as I pressed my hands against his hard, rippling muscles. He deepened the kiss, exploring, taking his time. I swore, he kissed like all those guys in the movies—hand on my face, fingers in my hair, perfect head tilt. Desire raged through my body. I wanted him so badly.

I tried to tell myself that I was using him. That if I ended up sleeping with him, it would be the ultimate blackmail. Because if his dad found out about us, Cole's college plans would be in jeopardy. It was the only leverage I had against him.

And while I would use that, the truth was that losing my virginity to Cole was one hundred percent for me. I wanted something to hold onto when the time came that Mom and I would inevitably have to run again, one perfect moment with the guy I couldn't stop thinking about—I even got a thrill out of our blackmail games.

He broke the kiss, and I sucked in a breath, tilting my head back as his lips trailed a path to where my pulse thundered at the base of my neck. When he eased back and met my gaze with dark promise swimming in his eyes, my body reacted, quivering with need.

I didn't want the separation between us and tugged on the back of his neck until he lowered his head and captured my mouth again. He took control, and I melted against him, loving every second. He drove me crazy.

Air was overrated—I could've kept going for another hour at least. When he broke the kiss again and his hungry eyes met mine, I stilled at the questions swirling in those captivating green irises.

"Are you a virgin, Riley?"

His voice was thick with desire, and I shivered. "Does it matter?" Because to me, it mattered less by the second.

"I want you, but yeah, I need to know."

Heat traveled up my neck to my cheeks and ears. I nodded. There wasn't any point in verbalizing it, but when he hesitated, inching back, I had to speak. "I want this, Cole."

His pupils dilated, and after a half second, he crowded me again. "Are you sure this is what you want?"

"Yes." I was ready, but that didn't mean I wasn't nervous. I needed to do it, if only to even the playing field so that we were on equal footing again—I hated him having the upper hand. Having sex with him would tip the scales in my favor. All I had to do was tell my mom what happened, and she would go to Cole's dad. Something about that felt like a splash of cold water, though. It didn't sit right. There were other ways to mess with him.

Most of all, I wanted him for myself, and I needed to unpack that—later and alone, as I replayed the perfect memory to take with me once Mom and I moved on.

With his hand at my waist, he backed me toward the bed then paused. Excruciatingly slowly, he trailed his fingers beneath my T-shirt then eased it up and over my head.

He'd seen me in a bathing suit before, but standing in front of him in nothing but a bra and a tiny pair of cotton shorts made me feel more vulnerable than ever. I trembled as a guttural moan slipped from his mouth. Then his lips were on mine again, and all the previous tension melted away. He took his time, exploring my mouth and teasing me while he eased my bra straps from my shoulders then undid the clasp with one flick of his fingers. My shorts and panties quickly followed. A rush of cold air hit me before he pulled me close. I shivered at the sensation of skin on skin.

His corded muscles flexed and bulged beneath my fingers as I trailed them over his chest, shoulders, and back. I gasped when he slid a hand down my stomach to dip between my folds and tease the sensitive bundle of nerves there. My stomach clenched hard, and desire pooled low in my gut. It didn't take long until I cried out from sensations exploding inside me as my knees buckled. He swept me up in his arms, depositing me on his bed before he followed, his towel in a heap on the floor. He made me feel small, delicate, and cherished.

I welcomed his weight then my head swam with need as his lips slanted over mine. His hand slid up the side of my body and over my stomach to cup my breast. With a gentle squeeze, my nipple stiffened. His lips left mine, trailing down my neck. When he sucked my nipple into his mouth, I arched against him, all nerve endings firing at once.

His moan vibrated against my skin, and he slid his fingers between my legs to tease my clit then dip inside. It was too much, and my body squeezed around his.

He paused to put on a condom then covered me with his weight. I felt completely alive with him, wanton and needy. When he pressed against my entrance, I gasped. He eased in slowly, letting me become accustomed to him. There was a slight resistance, and he paused, holding still as he devoured my lips, making me dizzy with need.

When he broke the kiss, I met his heated gaze, taking note of the strain on his face as he held still. He held himself in place inside me, seeming to read what he felt there to make sure I was ready, and my heart swelled. I felt safe in his arms, along with something else. *Trust*. Shock rippled through me at the realization just as he pushed deeper, and I tensed from the sharp sting of pain.

He didn't move but tensed, his muscles flexing beneath my palms. Instinctively, I knew when I was ready and tilted my hips up, craving the friction and fullness.

He buried his face in my neck, inhaled my scent, and whispered my name, his attentiveness increasing my desire for him. Every movement stirred my need for him until I writhed beneath him, urging him on, meeting his rhythm with my hips and arching my back so that his body hit my clit. Each powerful thrust brought sensations cresting in waves until stars burst behind my eyelids, and I convulsed around him so hard that I almost lost consciousness.

His moan vibrated against my skin, and it wasn't long before he chased my climax. We didn't speak as he shifted to the side, withdrawing from my body. He pulled me into him, and I relaxed into his warmth as we regained our breath.

My lips curved into a satisfied smile, and I couldn't help but think that my maid duties were officially done. What we had just done canceled the agreement.

I tilted my head against his arm, taking in his mussed dark hair that begged my fingers to run through it. Intense emotion burned in his eyes, and I wondered if they mirrored mine.

Something clicked inside me: *this is where I'm supposed to be, in the arms of the only guy who makes me feel more than what's comfortable.* I relaxed, enveloped in his embrace, and tangled my legs with his. It wasn't long before I dozed.

41

CHAPTER SIX

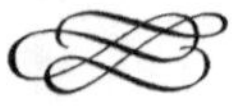

COLE

My blaring alarm pulled me from the best sleep, and I opened my eyes just enough to see my phone. I slapped the button, stopping the noise. I turned to my side, reaching for Riley, but the sheets were cool to the touch where she'd been.

I buried my face in her pillow, inhaling her sexy lilac-and-honey scent, and my body reacted instantly. So much for getting her out of my system. It took another minute to adjust to her absence. Another round this morning would have been nice.

I shoved off the covers then dropped my feet to the floor, resigned to how addicted I was to her. *What the hell am I going to do about that?*

She wasn't staying, and the faster I got her out of my system, the better. She was a grifter, and by the time I got all the information I needed and took it to my dad, she would be gone. That was what I wanted—at least it should have been. I needed to get my head on straight.

I stood then went into my bathroom to shower. As the water heated, I replayed every moment with Riley. She was wild and fiery, and I couldn't get over how she felt or moved beneath me. Everything about her was a fantasy. *I'm her first.* She gave herself to me freely and more than once because she wanted to, but she also took control of her own pleasure, which turned me on even more. She had been completely genuine and so damn sexy.

I took a quick shower and got dressed with her on my mind the entire time. Maybe, I thought, we could strike a deal and enjoy each other at night, putting all conflicts aside with a truce once we were in bed together. The rest of the time would be fair game.

Maid duty was over. I had a better way to occupy her time.

The more I thought about that idea, the more I liked the sound of it. Decision made, I tried to put her out of my mind.

It was Sunday, but I still had to get a workout in and determine who was going for a run with me. Phoenix was always game, and we would drag our brothers along, even though they preferred to sleep late. Leaving my room, I glanced across the hall to find Riley's door open and her bed made. Maybe she was getting breakfast.

I went downstairs and into the kitchen, phone in hand, and shot a text to Phoenix, intent on grabbing some water and a piece of toast.

"Good morning, Cole."

I stopped short at Raelyn's voice. She sat at the table, a mug of coffee in front of her, dressed casually in yoga pants and a T-shirt, her hair in a messy bun like Riley wore. I saw the appeal that my dad had fallen for—and he had, hard. It was unusual. Dad had delivered the threat about not messing with Riley with an intensity I hadn't seen in a while. Then there was the way he looked at Raelyn and how he watched her when she wasn't looking. Not that I was around them much, but I'd still taken notice. Not once had he been that way with Mom.

I grunted in response before grabbing a glass and filling it with water, my appetite gone. After chugging it, I put the cup in the dishwasher and turned toward the garage. I would just meet

Phoenix. A text to my brother was the best I could do right now. He would join us or not. That was on him.

She took a sip of her coffee, observing me over the rim before setting it on the table. "Do you want breakfast?"

I paused in the doorway. She seemed like she wanted to talk, and I had questions. I leaned against the doorjamb. "No, thanks. I'm going for a run. Where're Dad and Riley this morning?"

"Your father had to go to the office for a few hours." Then she smiled, and the sheer happiness of it hit me hard. "Riley is at diving practice." She blinked a few times, a sheen of mist coating her eyes.

Why is this such a big deal? "On Sunday?"

Raelyn shrugged. "I guess. I don't know much about when that stuff happens, but she told me this morning that she'd talked to the coach, and he said to come at six for practice."

Riley joined a team. Interesting.

"It's a big deal for her because she doesn't let her guard down with people. It's the first time she's ever joined anything." She grabbed her coffee and took a sip. I got a distinct feeling that she wanted to say more but stopped herself.

I didn't say a word but waited to see if she would share whatever else was on her mind. I noted how her leg bounced under the table, and her hand trembled as she tucked a few loose blond strands behind her ear. Something was bothering her. *Is it Riley letting her guard down?*

"Have you seen anyone new around town?"

"No." *What does that mean?* "Are you expecting someone?"

"Oh, no. I just thought I saw someone suspicious and wanted to see if you had." Raelyn shook her head then jumped up from the table, a fake smile curving her lips. "It's nothing. Have a great run."

I watched as she set her mug in the dishwasher. She was hiding something. I needed to call the PI and see if he'd learned anything.

My phone vibrated in my pocket, and I checked it as I headed out. Phoenix was already waiting in front of the garage, stretching. I joined him, my mind going a million miles a minute.

"Let's do a long run to the school. If we don't want to run back, we can get our lazy-ass brothers to pick us up."

"Damon wouldn't get up?" He finished stretching then stood, waiting for me.

"I guess. He didn't respond to my text, and I'm not going to chase after him. Where's Shane?"

"Tracey's parents are out of town, and since Mom worked last night, he spent it at her place."

I finished stretching, and we fell into a good pace, heading out of our subdivision and toward the high school. Five miles would give me plenty of time to think. "Did you know the dive team practices on Sunday mornings?"

"No, but they have a meet tonight, I think, and later this week. Maybe they're squeezing an extra one in."

That had to have been it. My phone buzzed with an incoming text, and I glanced at it. "Damon said he and Shane will meet us back at the house in two hours to lift." They liked to take Sunday as a rest day for cardio. I disagreed, but Phoenix and I were more ambitious about our goals, and reaching those goals took dedication, planning, and hard work. Thane University was the next step.

I set the pace, and we fell into a companionable silence, the distance melting under our shoes. It gave me time to think, which wasn't a great thing after spending the night with Riley. No matter how many girls I'd slept with in the past, being with her had been different. Primal. Something about her called to me, and I couldn't get her out of my head.

A physical relationship between us could work. It was just during the light of day that things couldn't. Her mom had to go, which meant she did too. Because our fucking dad would not get what he wanted—nor would Raelyn. They'd already destroyed Mom's life. It was their turn to suffer.

I would call the PI back after lifting to see if he'd found anything. Knowing Wes, he'd dug up information that could take them down. They were hiding a past that needed to be exposed, especially after the two encounters with the uncle and Raelyn's strange question about spotting anyone unfamiliar around town.

Our pace increased, but she still took up all of the space in my head. She pulled me to her like a magnet. When we were within a block of the school, we decreased our speed to cool down. Phoenix's phone rang, and we stopped in the grass by the side entrance to stretch. He flashed me the screen before answering. It was his mom.

"I'll be right back."

Phoenix nodded before I went to the athletic door that would have been unlocked if a practice was going on. I pushed on the door, found it unlocked, and headed to the pool. I'd seen her dive before, and there was no doubt that the coach had also witnessed her talent and pursued her to join the team. Not that I watched the divers or went to their meets, but when she'd soared through the air with complicated twists and turns, I knew I was witnessing something truly great, far better than most high school dive team members. That girl had her own destiny, and too bad—or not—it didn't align with mine.

I tried to convince myself that I was there to find out if she'd lied to her mom. But the truth was, I couldn't stay away.

I pushed open the door, and a wall of humidity hit me in the face, as it had the first time, when I'd spotted her there after hours. I walked between the bleachers then paused at the end, almost out of sight. The coach was in the office, talking to one of the swimmers with the door open. Someone jumped off the board. Not her. A few people congregated along the side of the pool, all in bathing suits.

Then I spotted her off to the side, chatting with Jarrett Duncan. I reacted before I realized it and stomped over to her, aiming a promise of retribution at Jarrett. He shrank back as my hand clamped around her wet arm and I yanked her away. I was furious, and I didn't even know why. But goddammit, she was not going to fuck me one night and indulge some guy who was making the moves the next morning.

I slammed my palm against the girls' locker room door then pulled her in with me and whirled around. "What the fuck do you think you're doing?"

She took a step back, fury pulling her features tight. "Excuse me? Take note, surface dweller, you have no claim to dictate what I do"—she jammed a finger into my chest—"or who I talk to."

I crowded her against the door and lightly wrapped a hand around her neck. Her pulse thundered against my skin, tempting me to close the few inches between us and kiss her. *Always with this girl.*

"That's where you're wrong." I kept my voice low, commanding. "You're living under my roof and sleeping in my bed."

"Once. We slept in the same bed one time." She flattened her palm against my chest and wrapped the other around my forearm.

"Once will never be enough," I growled, leaning closer.

Her pupils dilated. "It was enough for me."

I laughed. "I call bullshit." With a wink, I released her then eased back before I gave in, pulled her into my arms, and kissed her.

Jolts of heat raced through me at the first touch of our lips, and I devoured her. Tangling my fingers in her wet hair, I angled her head while her tongue danced with mine. I swallowed her breathy moan. Desire burned between us, and I knew that if I didn't break the kiss, things would go too far in that locker room.

I tore my mouth from hers and stepped back to put some necessary space between us while we worked to regulate our breathing. She met my gaze, her brown eyes burning. The girl could bring me to my knees with one touch. She made me crazy. I backed away then turned for the door to the hallway, leaving her standing there.

The door clicked shut behind me. The halls were empty, and I ran my hands through my hair, my need for her barely checked.

I knew I didn't have a right to control her, but because of the bullshit going on with my dad, I would do it in spite of wanting a different outcome. That was what angered me the most. Riley had pulled me in just as Raelyn had with Dad.

I texted my brother to bring my car and have Shane come, too, so they could drive home with Phoenix. I went to find him to relay the same message, and then I would wait.

Riley made me crazy. I shoved away from her. *I'm not my father*.

I couldn't put it off any longer. I headed for the exit door at the end of the hall. It was time to talk with the PI and get things moving, ending Riley's hold on me.

CHAPTER SEVEN

RILEY

ole is insane. Fucking psychotic to think he owns me even a little or that he can tell me who to talk to or who not to. Nothing was satisfying about dealing with that particular brand of jealousy. A spark of warmth followed the thought, but I squashed it, repeating that the alpha possessive side of him was not at all sexy.

I leaned back against the locker room door, not ready to go out and face the others after Cole's assholery. *What possessed me to sleep with him?* He was a control freak, and I shuddered to think that I had fallen into bed with him, given that caveman stunt back there.

Goose bumps rose and multiplied, and I crossed my arms over my stomach. *Wonder what he would do if I told Mom about last night?* If I let her know he was behaving like the complete neanderthal that he was, she would go to Lucas, and Cole would get a taste of his own bullshit for once. Or I hold it over his head, which would give me a strong advantage. Both of those ideas felt wrong in a way. *Stupid emotions.*

The bite of my nails against my palms startled me. I hadn't realized I'd made fists. Cole drove me crazy. But the worst part of it all, from the moment he'd kissed me last year to the present, was that I'd felt something real. It wasn't normal for me. I kept my emotions locked up, never truly getting involved with anyone. With one kiss, he'd broken through the wall I'd erected for as long as I could remember, *and look at me now.*

The door bumped me forward, and I moved away as Jasmine peeked around the corner. I gave her a half smile and headed for my locker. "Practice over?"

"Yeah." She went to hers and opened it, pulling out her clothes. "Are you okay? I'm not sure I've ever seen Cole react like that before. Not to a girl, anyway."

"I am, thanks. I don't know what his problem is." I shrugged and got my clothes out. The rest of the girls filed in. "Guess he doesn't like Jarrett?"

Megan snorted as she dropped her towel and grabbed her shampoo. "I think the real question is about you and Cole and what's going on there. Because that looked like jealousy to me."

I scowled, not wanting to give anything away. It would have been nice to have more friends, but I didn't know them. I made a mental note to ask Cassie about them to see if they were back-stabbing bitches who were friends with Piper and her crew.

I let the subject drop by pulling my toiletries from the locker and heading to the shower. After washing my hair and getting dressed, I hurried from the locker room, but not before Jasmine called out to me to remember we had practice the next day, early in the morning before school.

I waved in acknowledgment. That was going to be an adjust-ment. I was more of a night owl than a morning person, but the team seemed pretty cool. I didn't show them what I could do. I'd watched them first and mimicked their dives. Still, the coach had paid extra attention to me, and the others had obviously noted it but didn't seem put off. I hoped I could get to know them a little before I did my thing for real.

The walk down the hallway to the exit was silent, and I

found myself alone with my thoughts. *What was Cole thinking?* Jarrett was only telling me about the cliffs at the cove and asking if I wanted to go there to dive sometime. I'd said yes because I knew how impressive the cliffs were, and diving there was better than the school's pool. We could do so much more there. Not only that, but it would be fun to dive with others who knew what they were doing. It had always been a solo thing for me, and I didn't completely shun the new experience.

It was still hard to open up, but I was trying. Mom had asked me to give it a shot when she'd told me we would be here all year and that it was the last time we would move. I knew better, though. All it would take was for Dad or someone in his employ to learn where we were. It weirded me out that she seemed so sure this place would be different.

I hit the bar on the door to go to the parking lot, and it opened with a squeak. My mind was spinning, and I knew I couldn't go home like that. I needed to go to the cove and dive some more. It was the only way to escape my thoughts and that intense urge to do something—what, I wasn't sure. But being unable to talk with Mom, dealing with real emotions about Cole, and the new things at school were a cyclone in my mind.

I lifted my head before stepping off the curb when a black SUV stopped in front of me with the passenger-side window rolling down. Cole was driving. No one else was in the vehicle.

"Get in."

"Hell no." I turned to walk around the back to get to my car.

"Riley," he growled, "we need to talk." He put the car into park and opened his door.

I rolled my eyes. "Oh, there's plenty I have to say to you, but it'll be more yelling than talking."

"That's fine. We both have things we need to say, but not here."

"Why not?" I crossed my arms over my chest. "You have no

problem saying and doing anything you want here. What's to stop you now?"

"Get in the car, Riley. Please."

Please? I paused because that was a first, and something I never thought I would hear from him. Before I could second-guess myself, I opened the door and climbed in. He shut his door too. "Where are we going?"

"The cove."

Huh. That worked for me. But I wished I had my suit on rather than in a Ziploc inside my bag. "My car's here. It would be better if I followed you."

He pulled away from the curb. "I'll bring you back after."

There was something in his voice that stopped me from arguing. Whatever. I had my phone with me if he decided to leave me there. I could never tell with him. He went from hot to cold at the snap of a finger.

We drove in silence, but given how his hand gripped the wheel and that muscle jumped along his jaw, I knew he was holding back from arguing with me. I crossed my arms and looked out the window. It was fine. I had plenty to say to him as well.

"I didn't like you talking to Jarrett. He's a player."

I snorted. "Takes one to know one."

We fell back into silence. I wanted to fight. It seemed he wanted to wait. I bit my tongue. Once we'd pulled into the parking lot at the cove, I grabbed my bag and flung the door open— there was no way I would be stranded if he did decide to take off and leave me there.

There weren't any other cars or people. We had the space to ourselves. Jarrett had mentioned coming here this afternoon, so I expected it to fill up later. It was early, almost ten in the morning. If I hadn't had to go to practice, I would still have been in bed.

Cole motioned to the smooth rocks at the water's edge a

little way from the sandy part of the cove. I dropped my bag and joined him. I pulled off my shoes and let my feet dangle in the water. It was warm, and I was tempted just to push off the rock and sink under the water.

"I'm different than Jarrett."

"You sure are." *Okay, we're doing this.* I shifted, pulling my right leg up and resting my cheek on my knee to watch his expression.

"Piper and I weren't serious, and I don't sleep around, not since sophomore year." He met my gaze without flinching. "I haven't hooked up with her since the end of last year."

I wanted to ask what that meant, but it was easier to remain silent because the whole thing was too heavy, and I was determined not to misinterpret him. I doubted he was confessing his love and exclusivity to me, not given how much he wanted to kick Mom and me to the curb. He looked over the water, no longer meeting my gaze.

"Jarrett was checking out your body in that bathing suit that hid nothing. It pissed me off."

"It's a full one-piece." I scrunched my nose. *What is he getting at here?* "The same thing all the other girls wear. And did you get a load of what the guys were wearing? Not hiding anything there, either."

"Not the point, Riley. I know what that guy was thinking and that he planned to make a move. But I'm sorry for overreacting."

I didn't tell him it was okay because it wasn't. I could handle myself, just like always. I swirled my foot in the water, watching the circular ripples. It was the first time he'd opened up to me since he'd found me talking to my uncle then admitted it wasn't me that he hated. It was his father.

It felt almost like I could confide in him about my dad. I'd seen him fight, and maybe there was a chance he could protect me if I needed it. Not that I would ever ask, but having someone else who knew how to handle themselves, besides Mom and me, was a big deal. "Why do you hate your dad so much?"

Cole leaned back on his hands. "I don't want to talk about him."

"What about your mom?" I waved away a bug that flew a little too close.

"She died about a year ago." His voice was flat, uninviting.

I didn't probe for details. "I'm sorry. I didn't know." If it had been my mom, she would have taken all the colors in the world with her. Even though things had devolved between us in the last few weeks, I couldn't imagine a life without her in it.

He turned to me with such intensity in his gaze that I felt the world tilt. The gently lapping water faded, as did the distant buzz of nearby insects and the call of birds as they circled above a tree in the cloudless sky. Time seemed to stop, the moment pregnant with expectation. I held my breath, waiting.

With his focus directed at me like it was, his presence filled the space, shrinking everything else until all I saw was him. I felt like prey caught in the gaze of a predator, but there was something else too. His eyes dropped to my lips, and I shivered in expectation.

He leaned toward me, and I mirrored his action until we were an inch apart. His breath fanned over me in a sensual caress. I licked my lips, and his pupils dilated.

Abruptly, he pulled back then jumped to his feet, the crunch of pebbles beneath his shoes loud in my ears. "We should head back."

I gasped at the loss of what almost happened—a kiss. The moment loaded, like it meant something. I didn't understand. I'd slept with him, literally and figuratively, just the night before.

Even so, it felt like so much more. Emotions were involved—an added complication.

What am I going to do?

CHAPTER EIGHT

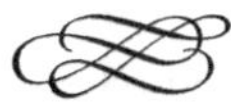

RILEY

"You know why." Mom's voice was tight with panic.

I entered the kitchen from the garage, practically on Cole's heels, and caught a small glimpse of the backyard. They'd left the slider open. She and Lucas were arguing near the pool.

Cole paused just out of their view, and I slammed into his back. He reached behind and steadied me before dropping his hand from my arm. Neither of us moved.

"We'll get it taken care of." Lucas stepped closer to Mom, cupping her shoulders with his hands. A tremor ran through her, and he caressed the side of her face. "Once the legalities are cleared, I want us to get married."

What the actual hell? My fingers grazed Cole's rock-hard back. His muscles bunched and prepared to spring into action. I wanted to fist the soft material of his shirt, but he wasn't mine. Lucas obviously wanted Mom in his life, and I knew everything would implode because she couldn't marry him. She was already married to my dad.

What he saw—loved—was all a façade: where we came from, our lack of extended family, our last names, and even the color of her hair.

"It can't happen." She shook her head as fat tears rolled down her cheeks. "He'll never let me go."

I sucked air, and Cole pressed me farther back into the hallway.

She told him about my dad—her husband.

There were rules—we never revealed our truth, who we're connected to, or what our real names are. *Never get attached.*

She broke the worst one. She broke them all.

I cringed. I was just as guilty... the diving team. The heat from Cole's body radiated into mine, and I rested my fingertips lightly on his back, keeping connected and warning him to stay there. I didn't want him pressing his body into mine again.

I couldn't decide which rule I violated more egregiously: emotional attachment or getting involved with the team. *We're screwed.*

Mom said my name, and I zeroed in on their bickering, letting my out-of-control thoughts fade into the recesses of my mind.

"Riley shouldn't have joined the team. If she's as good as you say, the media will be all over her." Lucas released Mom and paced along the edge of the pool.

Her voice hardened. "You said we would be fine."

There she is. I knew that version of Mom well. We kicked ass and took names. A sliver of calm eased the panic back. Maybe she wasn't emotionally involved, and I was the defective one.

"My sons will have her back at the school." He sounded distracted. "She'll be fine there."

Mom snorted. "Lucas, you really think your sons will have Riley's back? They blamed the party on her when she doesn't have any friends here. Certainly not the hundred or so who were in the house for that party. That smacks of your kids, not mine."

Lucas turned, a frown marring his features. "I already apologized to her."

"But you didn't punish your boys." She crossed her arms over her chest, challenging him.

"It was one party, and with all the changes, I didn't feel it was necessary. They've been through enough without me coming down on them for every little infraction."

Mom looked to the sky and softened her voice. "I know what they went through when their mom died."

"I'm sorry for what I put you through." He tried to pull her into his arms, but she turned at the last second.

"Yeah, I was the one left holding the bill for the hotel when you rushed home to her."

"The boys—"

Cole lurched forward. "What is she talking about? What hotel?" Then he was in front of his dad, flexing his muscles even more. "Or are you talking about the convention center?"

I rushed their way, my gaze darting between the three of them.

Cole knew. I could tell by his granite expression.

"Son—"

Cole's fist connected, and Lucas's head snapped back. I winced. Mom shrieked. Before Cole could hit him again, Lucas shoved him back. Cole caught air, and his head clipped the corner of the coffee table on the patio.

Damon rushed out. "What the fuck?"

Mom was at Lucas's side, checking his face as he stared at Cole with somber eyes. Cole gained his feet, and Damon grabbed his arm. Blood trickled down Cole's neck, and I rushed to his side. Head wounds bled, but still… "That may need stitches."

Cole cleared his throat. "Raelyn is the woman Dad was fucking that weekend." He never looked away from Lucas as he delivered the news to Damon.

"What weekend?" Damon growled.

Then Cole turned to me, and I had to dig my heels in not to flinch. But I would not cower.

"Did you know?" His voice was low and lethal.

"No." But the pieces were falling into place. *Mom's job last summer. Our short stay here and the crying she'd tried to hide from me.*

Cole sneered. "Get the fuck away from me."

"I swear I didn't know." I could feel the connection we'd had at the cove slip away. He wouldn't even look at me.

He got up, and as one, he and Damon headed to the gate. "I can't be in this fucking house anymore with these liars and cheaters." He snapped his piercing gaze to his dad. "Might as well be murderers."

<hr>

Cole

Damon and I went to our cousins' house. Staying at ours wasn't an option. I couldn't guarantee there wouldn't be another altercation with my dad.

I knew enough about Raelyn that she should have been forced to leave, but Dad was blind. *Marriage. What the actual fuck?*

Calmer, I pressed my phone to my ear, willing the PI I'd hired to pick up. I wanted to nail that bitch so Dad kicked her out.

He answered immediately. "Wes here."

"Hey, Wes. This is Cole Savage. Have you found anything on Raelyn and Riley Matthews?"

I could hear him tapping on his keyboard. "I was going to call you this afternoon. Their trail is muddy, probably deliberately. It looks professional. It's gonna take some time to pull the threads together, but I do have one thing established."

I leaned back in the desk chair in Phoenix and Shane's study room then glanced at the door to ensure it was locked. Riley tended to go wherever she wanted, and I wouldn't put it past her to follow me here and barge in.

"I talked with some tenants and the landlord about the address on Raelyn's driver's license when they were last in California. Your dad's firm employed her, but only for two weeks. After that, they moved to Vermont and used a different name."

Sitting straight, anticipation crawled over me. This was the stuff I needed to use against them. "What were the names?"

"Elise and Kinsley Ferrero. Raelyn, or Elise, worked for a large event. Kinsley volunteered. But by the time it closed, they were long gone. So was about twenty grand."

"They run cons?" The first day of school popped into my mind, when Riley lifted my wallet with such ease.

"Yeah, they're grifters. And damn good at it. They change their appearances and stay off the radar as much as possible. I barely recognized them."

"Including social media?" I'd overheard Raelyn ranting to Dad about the picture I'd taken and posted.

"They have no digital footprint whatsoever. The only reason why I was able to see what they looked like was because I got a copy of the fake driver's licenses they used. Someone wiped the electronic file in human resources. They either have someone helping them cover their tracks, or they're that good."

"Thanks, Wes. Keep me updated if you find anything else."

After he hung up, I sat straighter, plotting the best time to drop their little bomb and run them out of town for good.

CHAPTER NINE

RILEY

Chaos followed Mom and me everywhere. We were basically on a perpetual roller coaster, and this was no different… but it *felt* different.

Everything happened at once. Cole and Damon left to stay with their cousins. Lucas stormed off to his study. And Mom and I were left to figure out what had happened.

Mom was a wreck. Tears streamed down her face, smudging her mascara under her eyes, and she visibly shook. Shoving my pain and confusion to the side, I gently grasped her arm and led her to the patio furniture. We sank onto the tan cushions on the love seat, and I tossed one of the pillows to a nearby chair for extra room.

I got comfortable and shifted so that I used the armrest and a pillow for back support to face her. "I need the whole story."

Because there was one. She'd only given me bits and pieces, and I needed to know everything. Things had escalated to the point where we should run. I couldn't see anything to salvage, and I worried we'd somehow destroyed Cole's family.

With shaky fingers, Mom swiped the wetness away, managing to wipe the tears but only smearing her mascara more. Bloodshot, swollen eyes met mine, and I braced myself. *This is it—no more lies.* Sincerity and determination blazed like a beacon in her gaze.

"I've told you there's history between Lucas and me."

"Right." I remembered the conversation clearly. They'd met when I was a few months old and had a brief affair before we had to disappear. Dad had found us, and it got bad. We'd barely escaped.

"Your father..." She shuddered. "If Ronan hadn't found me, I wouldn't have survived that encounter. He helped us change our names again. And we disappeared. It broke my heart to leave Lucas the way I did. No note. No explanation." She closed a hand around mine, and I felt the connection in my bones. "But you were more important. And your father wasn't sure you were alive. I told him I had miscarried. I needed to keep you hidden."

I knew the story well. A nurse tied to the syndicate my uncle worked for owed him. She delivered me in the apartment where Mom had gone into labor. There was no hospital, no record of my birth, no paper trail to connect me to him. My identity was fake. The only way he ever would have known was through Mom, and she'd agonized over us having the same last name. We hadn't for years—not until I went to school for the first time. At each subsequent school, Uncle Ronan had worked his magic with fake paperwork, a new name, and fabricated transcripts.

In a sense, I was a ghost.

But there was a note, the one I kept hidden behind the picture of Mom and me in the frame on my dresser. A vile promise. A reminder of our future if he captured us.

The life we led wasn't a game. It was survival. And Mom needed a push to remember that because Lucas was her kryptonite.

A tiny voice in my head whispered that Cole was mine.

"Lucas searched for me all those years."

I remembered that part too. "He found you last summer. It's why we moved here." And my first kiss with Cole, the son of the love of Mom's life. If I'd known then what I was getting myself into, would I have stayed away from the party? *Probably not.*

"Yes. We moved here because Lucas asked me to." She shifted to mirror how I sat. "He was married."

"I remember." She'd carried a rose into the dump we'd rented one day, wearing a dreamy look in her eyes I'd never seen before. I'd overheard sex. *Gross.* "We didn't stay long."

"Lucas wasn't happy in his marriage."

I rolled my eyes. "We ran a lot of cons, Mom. But married men? They were off-limits."

She nodded very slightly. "I know." Her voice quieted. The tears had almost dried up. "He got married months before our affair and told me it was a mistake. But that's not my story. It's his. Last summer, I was at that legal convention with him. His boys arrived to deliver a note to Lucas from their mom. I didn't think they saw me because Lucas stopped me from turning to look at them. He asked me to wait for him in another room, but I stopped and turned as he read the note." She sucked in a shaky breath. "His face... I knew something terrible had happened. He ran out and left me at the damned conference."

"We didn't leave because Dad found us that night, did we?"

"No." Tears ran unchecked down her cheeks, and she stifled a sob. "Lucas called. It was brief. Something had happened, but he didn't go into details. He told me the boys needed him, and it wasn't the time to introduce me into their lives."

Another name change, another new city. "What made you give him a chance, move back, and try for the third time?"

Panic flashed through her eyes. "Your father was closer than ever. It was time to get help."

I jerked back, not liking where this was going. "Uncle Ronan helps us."

"Yes, he does. But things are changing, and you'll be going off to college soon. It was time to do something different. I want you to have a life without Nick breathing down your back."

My eighteenth birthday was a month away. The handwritten note Dad left for Mom swam into my mind. His threat for that day. "What could Lucas possibly do that Uncle Ronan hasn't already?"

She leaned forward. "Lucas has connections."

"So does Uncle Ronan."

"Yes. But this time, I want a different outcome. Not a war between syndicates." The corner of her mouth turned up. "Well, I wouldn't be opposed to a shootout where he dies, but there is another way to handle things."

"So why Lucas?" I wasn't clear about how she thought he would protect us better than Uncle Ronan could.

"I contacted him when we were in Vermont. I'd gotten word from Ronan that Nick was making arrangements for your birthday. There's a contract."

Fuck. Bile climbed my throat.

Mom jerked forward and grabbed my hand. Dark promise flashed in her eyes. "It will not happen. I won't let him get to you. I promise, Riley."

I wanted to believe her, but the bruises last time he'd found her flooded my mind, and I shuddered.

"Nick was close. Enough time passed after the boys' mom died. And I took a chance. Lucas was receptive to us moving back here. The house we stayed in—"

"I stayed in." Because Mom was never there.

"Right." Red infused her cheeks. "Sorry about that. Lucas and I were ironing things out. It was his house. We weren't paying rent."

Yeah, I'd found that out from Cole. It would have been great to have known that ahead of time so he hadn't blindsided me with that little tidbit.

"Lucas knows powerful people. If your dad—"

"When. Let's be real here." I was tired of half-truths and Mom's recent rose-colored glasses casting a hue that belied the truth. "You *told* him." The rules. *Her* rules. She'd broken them.

"I had to." She pressed her mouth into a tight line. "It'll be okay, Riles. I know it will be."

"It won't. We're destroying his family. The fight they just had." I flung my arm out to show the drops of blood that marred the patio. "Cole and Damon left. They went to their cousins'. Do you think they'll be back? I don't. Not while we're living here."

Mom stood and paced, her movements jerky and off-kilter somehow. "I never meant for the boys to find out about me this way. We never meant for them to find out at all."

I sank my teeth into my bottom lip, rolling it back and forth before releasing it. "We should go." *Cole will never look at me the same way again.* Things weren't great between us anyway. Only recently, he'd shown me what could be between us if he let go of his hatred for his dad. I didn't know if he would see me as anything but a pawn, and I couldn't blame him. I would have been equally as hurt if our roles had been reversed. Maybe more.

"Lucas won't forgive us for this." What I meant was that he wouldn't forgive Mom. "He'll become resentful if we're what keeps his sons away. We don't have a choice, Mom. We need to leave."

She tangled her hands in her hair before dropping them back to her sides then sliding onto the couch again. "I need to talk to Lucas, and I'll think about what you've said."

The way her voice softened when she said his name tugged at my heart. We'd both broken the rule of never getting involved. I worried that would cause our downfall. But I wanted to give this to her. Since day one of my life, she'd existed to protect me. Lucas was her dream. I could hear it clearly in how she spoke and acted around him.

"I don't want to talk about this anymore. It'll get sorted."

Will it? I don't see how. This is a mess.

"How did diving practice go? Do you like the coach and the team?"

I got whiplash from the change of topics. "It was different. The coach is fine. So is the team."

"I'm so excited for you. There's a meet coming up soon? The end of the week?"

"Yeah, then, but also later tonight. Was this what you and Lucas were fighting about when Cole and I came in?"

Some of her excitement faded. "It was part of it. He's worried it's too soon. He wanted to schedule a private meeting with you and the coach from Thane so you could show him what you can do without any publicity."

My mouth fell open. "Are you kidding me? That's…" *Generous. And so much safer.* "Then why did you tell me to go out for the academy's team?"

She tucked some of her hair behind her ear. "Because you've never had a normal experience at school. I wanted you to have this year to acclimate before college."

"Mom, I don't need that. I can acclimate anywhere." *I'm a fucking chameleon.* I could only shake my head in confusion. "You're acting like I've haven't infiltrated any group I wanted to get the information on our marks." *This is such a risk.*

"Lucas is working on making it safe for us." The head tilt with her chin lifted told me her stubbornness had kicked in, regardless of the steady stream of tears. "I want you to have this, Riles."

"It's not going to work out. This kind of thing isn't meant for a girl like me." I wished it was and that I could have this one thing. But since I couldn't… I'd had enough of living a lie.

I tilted my head ear to shoulder until a satisfying *pop* relieved the tension. Too much stress had built up in my neck from the unfamiliarity of what I was about to do. Sure, I could assimilate into any situation fairly seamlessly. But a meet where I was going to be true to myself and what I could do was different.

It made me vulnerable. Exposed.

Not only that, but I was going to do a complicated dive I knew the others on the team couldn't do. There were a couple of scouts there—Coach had pulled me aside and let me know. He'd called them for me. Said to go all out. So I would, but that didn't mean I wasn't a bundle of nerves.

I would draw attention to myself, even though I'd been taught not to do that since I learned to walk and talk.

I glanced at the stands and found Mom sitting there with a huge smile on her face. She looked like she was about to combust with nervous excitement. I scanned the people around her. Lucas was there, but I didn't see Cole, Damon, or their cousins.

That's good. Right? Yes. I needed to stop thinking about him.

I scanned the audience and those milling about around the stands. I'd checked before the meet and found out that there was a school paper, and they usually had someone covering the events. A deeper search got me the names and photos of the students on staff. As my gaze crawled over the people, I found one of them, Skylar McCormick. Dressed head to toe in black, she leaned a shoulder against the side of the bleachers, a camera hanging around her slender neck. Black hair fell to her shoulder blades, and she hid her stunning face behind large black-rimmed glasses.

I hurried over, pasting on an easygoing smile. "Hey. Skylar, right?"

She leaned back against the railing, raising one sculpted eyebrow. "Yeah."

I wanted to laugh. This chick was tough, and I liked her on principle. "You're taking pictures for the school's paper?"

"Sadly. Let me guess. You're looking for an exclusive? Maybe a front-page article?" She smirked. "That'll be tough. The football dipshits rule here."

My fake smile turned into a real one. *Yeah, this girl is my people. She just doesn't know it yet.* "That's the last thing I want. Article? No problem, and I don't care where it's placed." I shrugged. "But the picture… I don't want any." My body tensed, and I couldn't stop the darkness of my past from sweeping through me like an unexpected and harsh rainstorm. I shut down my expression, hoping she didn't get a glimpse of anything.

Sky straightened, her penetrating cornflower-blue eyes boring into me, seeing more than I wanted her to. Something swirled over her features, and I felt a connection born of hardship and fear that I hadn't experienced with anyone since arriving in that overprivileged town. "I got your back. No headshots or full views of your face."

My body sagged, and I had to reach out and steady myself against the railing, not even caring that she noticed. "Thanks. I owe you."

Coach called for me, and I hurried away. The meet was starting. I went to stand by Jasmine and Megan. The coach had me going last, which was probably for the best. Then I could get out of there rather than talk to anyone. I'd already told Mom, who said they would meet me by the car.

The meet progressed agonizingly slowly. It was the first time I'd been to one instead of watching professional competitions on video or TV. Before long, though, it was my turn, and I was too aware of the audience as I climbed the ladder. At the top, I stopped and blocked them out, clearing my mind and visualizing what I wanted my body to do. I was going to do a reverse one-and-a-half somersault with four-and-a-half twists.

Once I pictured it without any mistakes, I took three steps to the end then jumped up and into the first somersault. My body rotated and twisted before straightening from fingers to toes and piercing the water. I had a couple seconds of complete solitude before I had to angle myself toward the edge of the pool and kick off, surfacing near the ladder to climb out. Complete silence was followed by thunderous applause and cheers. Shock rippled through me, and I almost slipped and fell back into the water. As soon as I was out, I hurried to where the other divers were, said a quick thanks to their congratulations, then told the coach I had to leave. There would be no second dive for me today.

It had been a mistake. I was way too exposed.

CHAPTER TEN

COLE

"Why do you keep checking your phone?"

Damon's dark smirk said he knew why. And goddammit, I couldn't give him an answer. I was checking my phone repeatedly because I was waiting for a text from Riley, as if I was some sort of lovestruck girl.

It scared the hell out of me. Because I did care, though I never wanted to. Sleeping with her was supposed to cure the need I had for her, but it hadn't. I wanted her even more.

Phoenix handed me a beer, and I took a long pull, ignoring the droplets that hit me when Shane dove into the pool. Aunt Cece woke from the commotion of us barging into their house. She came down the hall, took one look at me, and forced me to take a seat while she examined my head.

I didn't care about the bump or the cut. The satisfying hit to Dad's face eclipsed any pain I might have felt. The cut wasn't bad enough for stitches, and she went back to bed, wearing a frown.

One good thing came of waking our aunt. She'd cleared us to stay there as long as we needed. Rather than disturb her sleep further, we moved completely outside and the farthest point away from her room.

"Now that you're calm"—Phoenix eyed me warily—"what's this about?"

I filled them in on what I knew. Raelyn was the woman Dad was screwing when our mom swallowed the pills and overdosed. "That's the real reason I wanted Riley cut off from everyone. If we got to her, we'd get to her mom."

"Isn't working, though, is it?" Phoenix dropped to the pool's steps and submerged himself to the top of his swim trunks.

Shane grabbed a Nerf football and threw a perfect spiral to him. They tossed it back and forth while Damon's stare bored into me.

"I heard you screwing Riley." He lowered his chin. Darkness flashed in his eyes. "Better get your junk checked for disease. No telling where she's been. Like mother, like daughter."

I set the beer and my phone down. "You better shut the fuck up. Riley's nothing like her mother."

"You're touchy about this girl who spread her legs so easily for you."

I got to my feet and was halfway around the pool before I knew what I was doing. Damon met me in the middle, and I launched my fist into his face. He blocked and retaliated. We traded blows, each one more satisfying than the last.

A hard shove to my side made me lose my balance. There was a splash. I was underwater. *What the hell?* I hit the bottom of the pool, righted myself, then launched to the surface at the same time Damon did. I growled and lunged.

"Stop!" Shane shouted.

Damon and I glared at each other before turning toward our cousins, who were obviously pissed. Both stood with hands fisted at their sides.

"You're already fighting with your dad," Phoenix said between clenched teeth. "You can't be fighting each other."

Phoenix was right. I focused on Damon, my fists balled underwater. I still wanted to pound him. "Riley's nothing like her mom."

"Fine. She isn't bad, but she's not wholly good, either." Damon frowned as he waded to the stairs and climbed from the pool.

I followed his lead, got out of the pool, and dropped into a chair. I'd kept the PI to myself, but maybe it was time to come clean. "There's more about Riley that I haven't shared."

He snorted. "Why am I not surprised?"

Phoenix and Shane each pulled up a chair, and I dove in, telling them everything I'd learned from Wes. How he'd found pictures of them in another state, their changing names and appearances, and finally… how they were grifters.

"So they're after your dad's money?" Phoenix's eyebrows furrowed. "Won't your dad make Raelyn sign a prenup?"

"Let her have his money. It would serve him right for everything he's done. Besides, our trust is protected." Damon's blue eyes flashed with dark intent.

"He would probably do a prenup, but that's not what I'm back and forth about. I have this information from Wes, and if I share it with Dad, he should kick them out."

"Should but probably won't." Phoenix leaned back in his chair.

"He seemed pretty into her when we were at your house." Shane grabbed one of the towels and slung it around his neck before picking up his beer for a long pull.

"Keep it to yourself." Damon crossed his arms over his chest. "This is Dad's problem. He's the one who cheated for years on Mom—"

"Nice to see you're finally on my side about them." I couldn't have kept the dryness from my voice if I tried. We got along about most things, but not any of this. It was mostly my fault as I'd tried to shield him from as much of Dad's cheating as I could. Unfortunately, it had backfired, and he thought Mom's issues were the root of their problems.

"I'm on the same page now," Damon snapped, "so let the pieces fall where they may. If she clears him out, he'll have something to think long and hard about. If Mom was still here, none of that would've happened."

"He's got a point," Phoenix, ever the voice of reason, said. "Besides, Raelyn has to be a damn good actress to pull it off, and I don't know… I've seen how they look at each other too. Maybe this isn't a con. Maybe it's real."

I hoped it wasn't. Dad was an asshole. If she took him down a peg or two, I wouldn't complain. "Fine. I'll keep it to myself." *For now.* And maybe, if it could work to my advantage, I would torment Riley with what I knew. It would be much better to have her around than in jail. My gut clenched at the thought of that happening, and I frowned.

"Ever notice how familiar she is?" Damon asked. "I think she worked at the Coffee Cabana for, like, one weekend."

"So?" I didn't see where he was going with that.

"It was the same weekend we lost our mom."

"What are you talking about? I've never seen Riley at school before."

"No." Damon dropped onto one of the lounge chairs around the pool. "She had black hair and a lot of dark eyeliner on. I only saw her at the coffee place that one time."

It couldn't be… A hazy image from a party invaded my mind, merging with that of the girl I'd dreamed about—our cousins' Fourth of July party and the girl who tried to swipe their dad's gold lighter. They wouldn't have cared if she'd taken it. But it was the principle of the thing.

I'd seen her. Under all that goth makeup and clothing, the girl was hot. I'd taken the lighter from her and copped a feel of that sweet ass while doing it. She'd challenged me, and I faced the gauntlet she'd thrown down.

The kiss. Even drunk, I knew it was spectacular.

I suddenly understood why there was something so familiar about Riley that I couldn't shake. Something wasn't adding up. The difference in appearance. Her being at the party. Then seeing her mom with Dad at the conference. Even the slight change to Raelyn's hair. Riley was the goth girl from last summer. *What game are they playing?*

What the fuck have I gotten myself into?

CHAPTER ELEVEN

RILEY

Lucas will pay for making Mom cry. The knob to his study was cold in my overheated hand. With a hard turn and push, I opened the door with force, and it smacked against the wall with a satisfying thud.

Lucas met my gaze, his blue eyes eerily similar to Damon's, and didn't flinch. He closed his laptop and leaned back. The chair squeaked in protest—he was a big guy.

He waited, not saying a word.

Fine by me. I had plenty to say. "I don't know what game you're playing, but it ends now." I crossed my arms and glared. "I'm only here by default because of Mom. She won't stay. You may think you can save us. You can't. You have no idea what's coming." Screaming at him wouldn't have helped, so I stopped before raising my voice. If I continued down that path, I might have given too much away, and that asshole already knew too much.

He rubbed his forehead. "I don't want your mother to leave, Riley. I love her. I fell for her seventeen years ago. I've never stopped searching for her, wanting her in my life. I will keep both of you safe."

I snorted. "You have a funny way of showing you love her." I motioned to him then circled the room. "You're in here, completely oblivious to Mom's pain—which, by the way, is temporary." We would be leaving this hellhole soon, before our past caught up with us. I felt the clock ticking like a live grenade with every cell of my being.

"I mean it. I'll keep you safe." His eyes blazed like Cole's did when he was heated over something—usually me. "Both of you."

My heart hurt, which was weird. Cole was gone and hated me more than ever. I needed to deal with it—I needed to forget him. The whole thing was ridiculous. I came in here to tell Lucas off, and I needed to stick to that then get out.

I clenched my jaw. "You won't. Those are just words. You may think you're powerful enough, but you're not. This thing you've got going on with Mom is just as toxic as what happened to her with my dad. You're cut from the same cloth: arrogant, smug, the kind of guy who uses women and throws them away. The only difference I can see is that you use money and emotion as your primary means of abuse, while dear old Dad uses the threat of violence as his primary means. But you both share emotional blackmail traits."

None of that was fair, but I had resolved myself to being pissed, and Cole's accusations said otherwise. I wanted to scream and threaten then run as far from this town and the men we'd encountered in it as I could. The problem was Mom. She didn't want to go. And she asked for so little.

Lucas stood, pressing his knuckles into the top of his desk as he leaned toward me. Before he could say anything, his phone rang. It was the distraction I needed. I whirled around and left the study as abruptly as I'd entered.

It wasn't supposed to be this way. Ever since we arrived last summer then again this time, things had been a mess. The connection between Mom and me was weird. It was as if I'd lost my best friend.

I raced up the stairs, barreled into my room, kicked the door shut, and launched myself onto my bed. The fluffy white duvet puffed around me then settled. *What am I going to do?* The anger dissipated enough for me to think clearly. What Lucas thought of my outburst didn't matter. I'd defended Mom, and that was what I'd set out to do.

I flipped onto my back and stared at the chandelier overhead, missing my old life more than I could bear. This world was different. There were pluses and minuses, and I liked some things… like the diving team. I knew who I was, and no one had discovered my weaknesses: my asshole sperm-donor father, the sense of betrayal and abandonment I felt because of Mom's relationship with Lucas, or the sheer loneliness of being unable to hang with her and talk about everything and anything like we always had.

Then there was Cole. What had happened in the kitchen? The explosion of emotions, Cole punching his dad, and then Lucas shoving him away were too much. Despite what he thought, I hadn't known about our parents' affair or how it had affected his mom.

Tears welled in my eyes, but I refused to let them fall. I let Cole get to me. There was something about him that I'd connected to for the first time in my life. I didn't know if it was because of how I'd grown up—fearing my dad, on the run, running cons with Mom—or if I was defective. I did know that I wasn't a mere shell of a person with him.

When he kissed me, I lost time. Nothing existed but the commanding way his lips moved over mine. My knees went weak when he held me, taking my weight as if it was nothing. Every part of me responded to him, melted for him. He was an addiction I couldn't quit. And I didn't think I wanted to.

I pulled out my phone and tapped his contact, which he'd programmed in my phone as *surface dweller*. I wanted to text him. All I could think about was him. I tossed it onto the mattress. There was no point. *He knows all about me now, and that's not a good thing.*

CHAPTER TWELVE

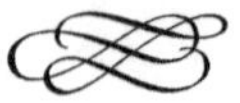

COLE

Riley is a liar.

I scrubbed a hand over my forehead. My brain hurt from the fight with my dad and her mom and the reaction on her face—her eyes had widened, and her jaw dropped in utter shock, and it conflicted with what I thought I knew.

I should call her. Text. Apologize.

But why? She lied. Over and over again.

She knew my mom killed herself—and it was her mom's fault. *And she acted like nothing happened.* My brain hurt. I went back and forth, sometimes believing she was innocent and didn't know everything about her mom's part in mine's death, who my dad was, and who I had been when they moved in.

I kicked my feet onto the coffee table, making Damon's beer teeter precariously. He swiped it, glaring. I lifted mine to my lips and took another long pull. Shane shouted at the football game on TV. Phoenix chimed in, momentarily distracting me, but not for long. Riley was embedded under my skin.

I couldn't just sit there after everything that had imploded earlier with Dad and Raelyn, especially combined with how betrayed Riley had made me feel. I needed an outlet to set some of the aggression loose. A glance at Damon told me he would be game. All we had to do was contact Snake and arrange a last-minute fight for that night. Because if I didn't do that, I would go crazy.

I downed half my beer while fisting my other hand at my side. Riley knew. A hundred percent. When I was losing everything, when Mom was dead and in a box, hers was busy fucking my dad. *There's no way she didn't know that.* Dad was a blatant and obvious cheater.

Dark intent filled me until it became almost unbearable. Hatred for my dad spilled onto her. It was inevitable. Thanks to Dad, I had to destroy Riley, even if I didn't want to. Besides, Mom would have expected me to take care of it. It didn't matter that she was dead.

Decision made, I couldn't wait for morning. Riley wouldn't know what hit her.

CHAPTER THIRTEEN

RILEY

Incoming—fight's over. Cass's text sent a devious thrill through me.

I hurried downstairs to the kitchen to enact payback for Cole calling me a liar earlier and for sneaking into my room and deleting the video. I'd recorded it the first time I'd gone to one of his fights with my phone hidden in my bra, only to slip it out when he was in the ring to document the illegal activity and use it as blackmail.

A last-minute underground fight had been set up, according to Cass, and she'd gone. I'd bailed, not feeling up for it after the explosion between Cole and his dad. The only reason I'd known they weren't at their cousins' house was because of Cass, who was wholeheartedly in on my plan.

Lucas was in the office, catching up on work, and the door was open a hair. That was enough. Mom had a newfound love of bubble baths, and I was pretty sure she was either in the tub or asleep. Either way, only Lucas would catch us, which was what I wanted to happen.

I grabbed a glass, filled it with water, then stood at the edge of the island, where he would get a full view. I knew what I looked like: just-fucked-hair, a tight T-shirt without a bra, and tiny sleep shorts. And I was well aware that after a fight, he felt primal and very sexual.

My heart pounded in anticipation, the kiss from the only fight I'd attended flashed through my mind, causing an overload of sensations. I wanted—needed—it to happen again.

It felt like forever, but I quickly heard the faint sound of the garage door. Leaning a hip against the counter, I took a sip of water, eyes half-mast, right when Cole opened the door.

His presence saturated the room, seemingly shrinking the overly large kitchen. Goose bumps raced along my arms, and my nipples hardened. Then our gazes locked and held. As his pupils dilated with intense emotion, I fought to maintain my pseudosleepy expression. I lowered my water and set it precariously close to the island's edge.

Cole closed the distance, and my pulse notched up another degree. He stalked me like prey, dark promise swimming in his green eyes as he advanced. I retreated but not by much. Just enough to goad him into pursuit.

In a lightning-fast move, his hand grasped my hip. He spun me around so my hips pressed against the hard stone countertop. My breath hitched at his touch as he tangled a hand in my hair. The other was like a steel band around my waist, drawing me close. Not even a millimeter of space existed between our bodies. Every hard ridge and groove of his body pressed against me. Then his mouth was on mine, demanding entry.

I clung to his broad shoulders, where the muscles shifted and bunched as he deepened the kiss insistently. His urgent caresses escalated my need. Desire raged between us. As he tugged on the hair at my nape, heat crested through me in waves from the hardness of him against my stomach. I was putty in his hands, my knees weak from the need he stoked to an unbearable pressure inside me.

There wasn't much time, and I feared I would lose track of it quickly. He would carry me to his room if I didn't do some-thing. I would have gone willingly, but I had a plan.

While I still had a modicum of brainpower, I slid my hands down his arms so that my left elbow was where it needed to be. With one sharp nudge, I felt the cool glass as I connected with it, sending it flying. Glass shattered, and my heart rate skyrocketed.

The noise didn't faze Cole. He tugged hard on my hair, breaking the kiss and angling my head for access to my neck. I gasped when he nipped me with his teeth, and my thighs clenched tightly against the throbbing between them.

Movement barely registered in my peripheral vision, but it was enough for some sense to trickle into my lust-filled brain. Palms flat on Cole's chest, I shoved. "Stop."

He growled, the rumble vibrating from his chest and into me. I shivered, my need for him impossibly high.

"Cole!" Lucas's deep voice cracked like a whip through the kitchen.

Cole's grip on me loosened, and I wiggled free then dashed to the stairs on legs that trembled almost too much to take me there. I didn't need to stay around for the fireworks. It was enough to know that he would answer to his dad. A pang of guilt pierced my hazy mind. I sank my teeth into my lower lip as I locked the bedroom door behind me and climbed into bed. He wouldn't get into too much trouble. It had only been a kiss.

CHAPTER FOURTEEN

COLE

*G*oddammit. *Worst timing ever.*

"Cole!" Dad's voice was like nails on a chalkboard cutting through my need for Riley, who had fled. "Turn around. I'm talking to you."

I braced myself on the island's cool stone countertop, thinking of anything that would eliminate how my dick strained against my zipper, trying to break free and find her. Christ.

I planned to find that little minx once I got Dad off my back. We had unfinished business. If I'd stayed at my cousins' place, not called a fight to dispel some pent-up aggression from the confrontation earlier, and waited until tomorrow morning to enact different plans for Riley, I wouldn't have been in that mess... although that kiss, as brief as it was, said I'd made the right choice to come home, regardless of my present circumstances.

After another few seconds, I regained enough control to face my dad.

Fury radiated off him. "My office," he snapped before whirling around, obviously expecting me to follow.

It was the only way to end whatever he wanted to rail at me about. Then I would be free to find Riley and get back to where we were.

"Close the door."

I obeyed then leaned against it, crossing my arms over my chest. My psyche warred between knowing I needed to let him rant and going upstairs and dragging her to my bed.

Dad paced several feet in front of me, in front of his desk. Unusual behavior for him. He was known for his intensity and composure before he went for the kill, both in the courtroom and in life. And he always did. His case record was something like ninety-nine percent wins. And I think the one loss was because he fired the client midtrial because of something he'd uncovered. I wasn't entirely sure of the details. They didn't matter much to me.

My gaze skimmed over the wall of legal texts behind him to his large mahogany desk, where he must have been doing some late-night work, as his laptop was open and a legal pad was beside it. The blinds were closed over the floor-to-ceiling windows to my left. There was a bar off the corner of the room behind cabinet doors. I had to stop myself from opening it, pouring a whiskey, and sinking into one of the leather club seats nearby.

I'd always liked his study, but I swore long ago that I would never follow in his footsteps. And I still didn't plan to, no matter how much he thought he could push me into getting a law degree and passing the bar exam.

I could see Damon doing it, though, maybe. He had the same cold focus as Dad and a knack for intimidating anyone into spilling their guts with one look. After I left, Damon would have another year of high school and plenty of time to figure out what he wanted.

Aside from football, I knew what I wanted, and nothing my dad did or said would sway me.

Dad stopped pacing and stood in front of his desk, glaring at me. "I thought I made myself clear about Riley being off-limits." His deep voice reverberated off the walls, demanding obedience.

But I made my own rules. "It was just a kiss." *For now. More later.*

"You're not going to screw this up for me, Cole."

The fuck? "Screw what up? This family? You've done a great job of doing that my entire life."

"You don't know what you're talking about."

"Enlighten me, then!" I forced myself to remain where I was so we didn't end up punching each other again.

He ran a hand over his face. I hated how alike we looked. "Raelyn means a lot to me, and if you mess with her daughter…"

I grinned, and by the emotion that snapped to a glimmer in his eyes, I knew that all the darkness I felt inside was reflected in my expression. "Maybe you should tell Raelyn that I've defiled her precious daughter. Wonder if she'll stick around or take off… again?"

He pressed his mouth into a tight line, and his body visibly tensed. *Come on, old man. Make the first move.* I wanted to keep goading him so he would come at me. I was more than ready to slam my fist into his face.

"I ask for very little from you and your brother. And my one ask was that you not enter into an intimate relationship with Raelyn's daughter."

I said nothing. It was too late for that, and there was no way would I stop. He tried to stare me down and took a deep breath when it was clear that I wouldn't budge. I knew a lecture was coming. I hated those—trying to win an argument with Dad was a lesson in futility. It was intellectually and emotionally exhausting, which I enjoyed when I had the time. I did not have that time.

He could make all the threats he wanted, but I knew him

well enough to know he wouldn't do any of it. He was one of the largest financial donors to Thane, and he had pull. Lots of it. And while I hated him for what he'd done to Mom, he had always been fair to Damon and me, at least for the most part. But that didn't negate everything in the past, and it never could. My feelings for him wouldn't change, especially since he'd brought his mistress into our house.

His daughter was another matter, though.

He briefly pinched the bridge of his nose. "If I have to move Riley into another wing of the house, I will. And if you continue to push the boundaries where she is concerned, I'll install a camera in the hallway. I'm very serious about this, Cole, and I expect you to do as I ask."

"Is that it?" I would neither confirm nor deny what I planned to do.

"For now." He glanced back at his computer. "Cole"—regret carved brackets around his mouth—"I apologize for shoving you. How's your head? Did Cecilia look at it?"

No way was I apologizing. My jaw hardened. "It's fine, and yes, she did." I should have stayed at Aunt Cece's with our cousins like my brother had... but I needed Riley.

Dad's phone rang, which surprised me because of the late hour. Riley and I must have interrupted something urgent if he was up this late and away from Raelyn, who was probably waiting for him upstairs. I opened the door and had one foot in the hallway when he spoke.

"And clean up the broken glass in the kitchen."

I froze, narrowing my eyes. So that was how he came to find us in the kitchen.

Riley set me up. She thought she had me. She couldn't have been more wrong.

It didn't take long to clean up the broken glass and water. And when I was sure my dad was engrossed in whatever work kept him from Raelyn's side, I went upstairs. I tested the doorknob to her room and found it locked. That wasn't going to stop me.

In my room, I got one of the metal keys that would fit into the small hole in the doorknob. Inserting it, I popped the lock and then stuck the two-inch metal stick into my pocket. In case she decided to launch something at my head, I eased the door open slowly. It was dark inside, but the moon was full, and I could make out her slight frame under the covers.

I stood over her, watching her chest's slow rise and fall beneath the blankets. Her long lashes fanned over her cheeks, and her eyes rapidly moved under her closed lids. Enough time had passed since we'd kissed that she could have fallen asleep. That wasn't a problem for me. For the next few hours, I planned to stay in her room. No way in hell would I sleep in there, though, not after the little stunt she'd pulled. Getting busted once was enough for me.

Just being in the same room with her made me hard. Sex was going to be fast and furious, as I was still pumped up after the fight and the tease of tasting her before arguing with my dad. Anticipation churned in my gut, and I tore off my clothes as quickly as I could, deciding at the last minute to put the condom on before climbing into bed behind her.

Warm, soft skin met my palm as I slid my hand beneath her sleep shirt and over her tight stomach, grazing the underside of her breasts. Fuck, she felt amazing. She stirred in my arms, and I whispered her name. When she turned her head and blinked sleepy eyes at me, my heart squeezed with an emotion I refused to recognize.

"Cole?"

I nibbled on her neck, her pulse jumping at my touch. "We were interrupted earlier."

I cupped her breast, giving it a gentle squeeze, and she squirmed against me. Her soft, sexy ass pushed back, and I met her with a slight thrust. My dick nestled between her cheeks. "You're wearing too many clothes."

She moaned, and I took that as a yes to slide her tiny cotton sleep shorts over her hips, exposing her skin to my touch. I wanted to taste every part of her, but a glance at the clock said it was already one in the morning. We had school in a few hours, and I didn't think I could hold back much longer anyway.

I held her against me, one hand giving her breasts attention as I slid the other down her abdomen and between her legs. My eyes rolled back in my head at the first caress. "God, Riles. You're so wet."

I loved that about her. She was incredibly responsive. Her need matched mine in every way.

I teased and played with her clit until she begged me to make her come. But I wasn't done. I slipped two fingers in, curled them, and pumped deeply. Riley shook in my arms, her hips meeting my every movement. Still, I held back, slowing my touch when she wanted me to go faster until cursed at me to give her more.

"Cole!" She gasped.

I moaned as I felt her body clench around my fingers. Replacing them with my cock, I surged inside, her body squeezing around me. It was fucking amazing. My fingers stayed on her clit, rubbing and spreading the silkiness of her come over her as I thrust as deeply as I could. But I wanted more.

She cried out when I withdrew. I got to my knees and leaned back on my heels before picking her up. Her legs automatically wrapped around my hips, and she held onto my shoulders as I lined up at her entrance. Hands on her hips, I guided her onto me. We both groaned at how good it felt.

Then she rocked against me, and it was all I could do not to toss her on her back, but the sight before me as Riley rode my cock was outstanding. She was gorgeous and so damn responsive.

It didn't take long until we both came. Collapsing onto the bed, I pulled her into my arms, unable to resist holding her for a few minutes. It took a minute for our breathing to regulate, and I wanted to sleep with her in my arms.

"What was that?"

A fierce possessiveness rose in me at the sound of her breathy, hoarse voice, and I wanted to take her all over again. But that wasn't how tonight was going to go. "That was damn good sex." I hardened myself against her wide eyes. "And that's all it was." She stiffened, but I was already rolling to my feet. I gathered my clothes and left without a backward glance.

I had to leave her room before I climbed back into bed and pulled her into my arms. I wanted too badly to hold her all night and feel her writhe against me all over again. And even though we'd agreed to call a truce at night, we still waged war during the day. Tomorrow, it was my turn to strike.

CHAPTER FIFTEEN

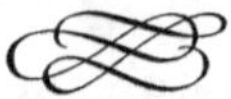

COLE

Hate beat obsession in my book. That was what I convinced myself about Riley. It helped me not think about her constantly—especially after what we'd done last night. I needed a distraction to keep it that way. I scanned the crowd in the hallway at school. Piper paused, her hand on her locker. Her eyes promised whatever I wanted. Too bad it wasn't her.

"Cole." She sidled next to me. "How was your weekend?" She didn't wait for me to answer. "I was thinking you could come over after practice. Or... I could go to your house?"

"No." I moved on. If I even thought to use her, there would be issues—and I had no doubt she would pick up on the even chillier reception I was giving Riley. Piper was too smart for her own good sometimes. For the past several months, I'd been trying to shake her, and I wasn't about to undo the work I'd done.

"Hey, Cole." Eliana stopped a foot in front of me, her gaze skidding from Piper, who was slightly trailing behind and back, to meet mine.

I took in her shiny blond hair and generous curves. She would do. I went up to her and threw my arm around her shoulder, pulling her to my side. She changed directions willingly.

Awareness tingled over my skin. Not from Eliana. For her, I felt nothing.

Riley was ahead, shoving her bag into her locker and taking out her physics book. Eliana was chattering in my ear, but I wasn't catching any of it. From the corner of my eye, Riley turned slightly, her long silky brown hair rippling over her back, stopping just short of her narrow waist. Faded jeans clung to her toned legs and hugged her ass. The shirt she wore stopped at the waistline of her jeans, giving me peaks of her toned abs when she moved. I clenched my teeth as I passed beyond where I could see her in my peripheral vision. No way would I let her catch me looking.

Anger continued to heat my blood as I bent and pressed my lips to Eliana's long enough that Riley saw. Then I was done with her. My hands fell away, and I walked into class without a backward glance. Eliana spoke, but I didn't care enough to listen.

Riley got the message. There was no way she missed that kiss, the one I couldn't even remember participating in a second ago. And for the next hour, she would receive the rest of my little wake-up call.

I took my seat across the aisle from hers. Tension crackled between us. It would only get worse. Mr. Gerritsen droned on about some experiment we were going to do. Riley stared straight ahead. Not once did she look at me, but I'd caught the heated flash in her eyes when she entered the classroom and took her seat. Even though she wanted me to think the kiss between Eliana and me hadn't affected her, it had.

It wasn't until the teacher called out lab partners that my

attention zeroed in on what he was saying. I must have heard wrong. "Excuse me, Mr. Gerritsen." A hush settled over the room.

Our teacher's small brown eyes fixated on me. "As I was saying, Cole. You'll partner with Riley—"

"No." It was another opportunity. I leaned back in my chair, crossed my arms over my chest, and kicked my legs out under the desk. "I won't work with her. I would be worried for the integrity of the project."

"I hardly think that'll be an issue. Riley's grad—"

"She's a grifter, and it's possible that she'll move on to the next town once she and her mother finish suckering some poor sap here."

Part of me cringed because I'd just hung Dad out to dry. But fuck him. He'd brought them into our lives.

Riley's palm slapped onto the top of the workstation as she turned to face me, her eyes promising retribution. "Listen up, Surface Dweller. I'm smarter than that. You and your delusional father can't hold a candle to my mom." She narrowed her eyes and lowered her voice. "And at least I've got one."

"Sto—"

"Another thing to lay at your mom's feet." I didn't let the teacher have a say. I needed to do this. I turned to her, enraged that she had brought my mom into the argument. "Or were you planning on spreading your legs for me so I'll do all the work? Like mother, like daughter?"

"Enough!" Mr. Gerritsen yelled. "Go to the principal's office. Both of you." He shot his arm toward the door. "Now."

I yanked my backpack off the floor and swung it over my shoulder. Someone cried out. I didn't look to see who I might have hit. Riley stormed out ahead of me, her book in hand. Her lilac-and-honey scent hit me as I fell in line behind her, ignoring the shocked faces and raised phones around us. When she smirked over her shoulder, I stepped closer, catching the door she flung back in my face. "Nice try, but not good enough."

We kept pace on opposite sides of the hallway. I didn't trust myself to get too close to her. Even angry, I wanted her.

The office was busy. We sat for a few minutes in the uncomfortable wooden chairs that lined the wall to the secretary's left before being called in separately. I went in first and got a slap on the hand. Principal Morris was an avid supporter of our team. All I had to do was steer the conversation that way after promising the incident with Riley was a one-time thing.

When I left, he called her in. The bell rang. I didn't need a pass and headed to my next class. My mind spun from our fight. Classes went by in a blur until lunch, where I dropped onto the seat next to Phoenix and across from my brother and Shane.

"So, physics class…" Damon grinned, and I stopped scanning the lunchroom for Riley.

"The whole school's talking," Shane said.

"Yeah." Phoenix tilted his head, regarding me like I'd grown two heads. "Hating Riley is back on?"

When I met his gaze, I flinched from how conflicted I was. It was Riley's fault and her mom's. They were the root of our losing Mom. Dad was guilty, too, but it was easier to lay the blame at their feet. "I never really stopped. She's a problem that we need to deal with." I was distracted, but I refocused on my brother.

"And to think it was only yesterday"—Damon smirked— "that you wanted to kick my ass for saying shit about her. But today, you're the one badmouthing her."

"I never should have let her in, not even a little."

Damon's features darkened to what he looked like before a fight. "After what went down yesterday, I would hope so."

I didn't hear what he said next because Riley walked into the lunchroom with Cass, who should have known better than to hang out with her. *And why aren't Piper and her minions all over Cass for that?*

"Brooke." Phoenix seemed to read my mind. "Remember she and Cass used to be friends?"

I nodded. Made sense. Cass must have gotten a pass for some reason. No matter, as long as everyone else gave Riley a wide berth. I tore my eyes from her and chugged the water I'd grabbed on my way in.

Phoenix stiffened. That was all it took for me to spot that asswipe from the dive team as he sat next to Riley. He cupped her shoulder and squeezed before his hand fell below the table. The fucker sat close enough that he might as well have been inside her.

I was standing before I knew it, fueled by insurmountable rage. The distance to their table evaporated beneath my long strides. Then I was in front of Jarrett, my hand fisted in his shirt as I hauled him from his seat. My fist connected to his face with a satisfying crunch.

There were screams. Shouts. Nothing would stop me from hitting the fucker again. Something wrapped my arm tightly, and I glared over my shoulder.

Phoenix had my bicep in a vise grip. "Not here!"

Shane grabbed my other arm. Damon stepped between me and the guy, whose face dripped with blood. My cousins pulled me back while I strained to get to him again. I needed another hit. He hadn't heeded my warning the first time, and I wanted to wipe the floor with him for ignoring it. Sure, she was hot as fuck, but to cross me meant retribution. And my reputation was well known.

Riley launched herself over the table until she was in front of me. Her palms smacked my chest, and she shoved. It was the only thing that made me stop struggling. Her cheeks were red, and I think she growled. But all I heard was my anger buzzing in my ears.

I stopped struggling to break free. She was livid, making me want to laugh in the silent lunchroom. Staff converged, and we broke apart, sent to the principal's office for the second time that day.

Wonder if I can talk my way out of punishment this time.

CHAPTER SIXTEEN

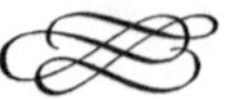

RILEY

That asshole got me suspended.

In all my quiet, don't-let-anyone-in, make-good-grades-and-stay-under-the-radar behavior, I'd never been suspended from anything partly because I was usually invisible—by choice. Not here, thanks to Cole putting a target on my back from day one, orchestrating everyone at school to ostracize me, and telling everyone they'd better uphold the freeze.

Cass had chosen to ignore it, exempt from retaliation because of Brooke. And Jarrett had disregarded Cole's edict when he sat beside me at lunch and gotten his ass handed to him for it.

Three-day suspension for fighting was what Principal Morris had decided was an acceptable punishment. I hadn't done anything—the total bullshit was all Cole's fault. His dad was giving off some furious vibes, which brought me a rush of satisfaction as we drove back to their place. I was angry too. So was Cole. The only one with other emotions was Mom, and she seemed worried.

Mom and Lucas were in the front seat with Cole and me in the back. I was glad the SUV was huge since we were stuck together. There was plenty enough space for his stupid long legs, so they didn't touch mine.

No one said a word on the ride home, and when we got to the house, I ignored them all and went to my room. Mom was too quiet on the drive, and more than once, I caught her looking at her phone. I didn't like it.

She'll come up. I just had to wait because of course she would come to my room. We could talk about everything then. I sat cross-legged on the queen-sized bed I was getting too used to. Mom had looked fearful when we got out of the car. It had to mean we were leaving. Probably tonight. *Good. I'm ready to go.*

I needed to pass the time and swiped my thumb across my phone's screen. Rolling to my stomach, I read through the shouty texts from Cass. The last one demanded that I respond. I laughed, and warmth filled me because she cared. I wasn't used to that.

My fingers flew over the keys as I gave her a quick recap of what happened after Cole slammed his fist into Jarrett's face. I couldn't believe he'd done that. Irritation flooded me all over again, and I glanced at the time.

Mom should have been up there by now. I couldn't wait any longer. Something could have been wrong. Three dots appeared. Cass was texting me back, but I needed to find out why Mom wasn't talking to me.

I rolled off my bed, landing on my feet, then crossed my room to the door, yanked it open, and burst into the hallway but stopped short. Cole leaned a shoulder against his open door, and I scowled. He looked pissed. I didn't care.

"I told you to stay away from Jarrett."

Fucker. I wanted to confront him, but I had to talk to Mom more, so I took the high road. When he opened his mouth to say something, I held up my hand, palm facing him, and snapped, "Save it."

I rushed down the stairs in search of Mom. Thankfully, Cole

didn't follow. When I didn't find her in the kitchen or the living room, I went to Lucas's study. It wasn't where I wanted to be, but something was up, and I wasn't going to be left out.

The door was cracked, and I could hear them talking in hushed voices. With my knuckles, I lightly wrapped against the wood. "Mom?"

"Come in, Riley," Lucas answered, and I frowned.

Why is she letting him talk for her? I pushed open the door but stayed where I was, taking in the scene. Lucas was standing at Mom's side as they both looked at something on her phone.

"Riley." Mom's face was ashen, and she dropped the phone to her side. "Is everything all right?"

"Stop, Mom. What's going on?" I didn't like this version of her and missed the old one. I shot Lucas a dark look, not at all happy he'd stayed in the room with us. "The truth." I glared at her fiancé for good measure. "And just the two of us for this discussion."

"I'll go talk to Cole." He kissed Mom's forehead and squeezed her arm before leaving us alone.

I stepped aside so he could pass, never taking my eyes off Mom. She held her phone out when he was gone so I could see the screen. I moved closer. I didn't recognize the number, but the message said everything.

Tick-tock, Rachel. She's almost 18.

My mouth went dry, and my body tensed. Rachel was her given name, not an alias. "We have to go. Now." Urgency made me rush my words. "If he hasn't found us, he will."

"I know." Mom closed her eyes for a moment. When she met my gaze again, determination and stubbornness blazed within. "We're staying. This is it, Riles. Lucas will help us, and we'll break free of him for good."

"How?" Horror surged through me. "In a body bag?"

She lurched from the chair and rushed forward to grab my hands. "No. It won't come to that. I promise."

Bile climbed my throat, and I frantically swallowed. "You know better than to make those kinds of promises." I dropped my voice to a whisper, not wanting to give the memory more power. "The last time he found you, we were almost too late. I relive those hours in my nightmares more than I care to admit. I don't want him to take you from me for good. Please, let's leave. Now. Or at least tonight."

"This is our best option. I'll reach out to Ronan and let him know what's happening, that your father is close." She cupped the side of my face, her features softening. "I want so much more for you, Riley. And Lucas is powerful. He'll help us take Nick down."

"No. Lucas can't save us from him. Mom, whatever hold Lucas has on you, please listen to reason before Dad does something we can't undo."

"Nothing bad will happen. Not this time." She squared her shoulders.

I didn't miss the slight tremble in her hands, though. I backed up, severing the connection. We'd done some risky things over the years, but staying here was the worst.

CHAPTER SEVENTEEN

COLE

Something strange was going on in the house. Everyone was on edge. Dad and the woman who might as well have killed my mother insisted that the alarm stayed on even when everyone was home. No one was saying why.

Edgier than usual, Riley swam laps in the pool. I wasn't the only one with energy to burn without practice after school.

The suspension meant no football. I wanted to hit Jarrett again. I needed to hit something—someone—and we didn't have any underground fights until this weekend.

Furious, I spent that night reviewing film of the team we would play on Friday. Coach had talked to Principal Morris, and as long as I went to practice on Thursday, I could play. I would be back by then, so there wasn't a problem.

It was the first day of our three-day suspension, and I'd already worked out and gone for a run. Homework took another hour. I thumped my head against the back of the couch. Damon, Phoenix, and Shane wouldn't be home for a few hours. The problem wasn't being bored out of my mind—I was—but more about keeping my hands off Riley. The way she'd felt in my arms, how she'd clung to me, and asked that I stay throughout the rest of the night when she'd had that nightmare played on repeat. I kept seeing that storm in the middle of the night when my dad and her mom were staying in the city. Things were crazy between us. It hadn't been long since I'd erased the video she'd recorded of my underground fight but before I'd caught her meeting with the man she claimed was her uncle. That night, we'd called a truce.

But Riley and I were still at war. As confusing as our nights and days were, I couldn't let them stay. Dad was way too comfortable with them becoming a part of our family. After a short lecture to both of us about keeping the alarm on at all times, he and Raelyn left for an early client dinner.

I felt like a caged animal. We were alone in the house. I wanted her and hated myself for it. When the doorbell rang close to the time school ended, a wave of relief crashed over me. I needed a distraction.

At the front door, I paused when I heard a splash. I glanced over my shoulder and saw her doing laps in the pool. A laptop was on the patio table, and the sliders were wide open. Guess I wasn't the only one not adhering to the alarm mandate. Or maybe she thought since the yard was gated, it was the same thing.

I yanked open the door to find Eliana standing with her hand poised to knock again. I skimmed her short skirt and form-fitting T-shirt and opened the door wider.

It was still hard to believe that I had zero interest in anyone other than Riley. *It has to be my obsession with running her and Raelyn out of town.* I ignored the other voice in my head that called me a liar.

"Why are you here, Eliana?"

She pushed her hair over her shoulders. "I heard about the fight and your suspension. I thought you could use some company. Maybe a way to relieve some stress?"

It was a bad idea, but I opened the door wide, and she

entered. With a mischievous grin stretching her mouth, she trailed a hand across my abs as she passed. I wasn't even a little bit interested, but—I grinned back—Riley might find Eliana's presence annoying.

I shut the door and led her through the house and into the family room, where I was honing my *Call of Duty* skills and switching to *Madden* when that got old. She sat too close on the couch, touching her leg to mine, and chattered about school gossip. It was perfect because I didn't need to say a word.

I stayed hyperaware for Riley's arrival. Every once in a while, I could hear the water splashing from her laps in the pool. It'd been a half hour at least since she went out there. *How much longer can she keep that up?*

Bored, I tossed the controller onto the couch and switched to a recorded football game. I leaned back, and Eliana plastered herself to my side, tangling one of her legs with mine. My irritation level spiked. I didn't push her away because the sounds in the pool had stopped.

"Maybe you should have a party." Her high-pitched voice shattered my focus.

"Probably not." My dad's patience was stretched thin. I didn't need to aggravate him more when I wanted him to take me seriously about Raelyn's deception. I'd called them grifters and was still shocked there had been no reaction on his part. *Does he know what they did?*

"Oh, okay. I guess that makes sense."

I wanted to shove her out the door. Of course, it made sense.

"Piper's having a party this weekend. Do you want to go with me?"

"I'll think about it."

"Did you hear that Jarrett threatened to sue? He didn't return to classes, either." She wrung her hands. "What are you going to do?"

I paused and studied her behavior. *Looks like she has a crush on Jarrett.* "He won't sue." My dad would take care of it, or I would chat with Jarrett and convince him to get over it while issuing another warning to stay away from Riley.

A shuffle sounded outside, and I glanced toward the patio door. Riley was gathering her things and heading inside. She had a towel wrapped around her body, hiding her curves. She spotted us, rolled her eyes, went upstairs, and slammed the door to her room.

It was all I could do not to shove Eliana to the floor. Since that kiss I gave her in the hallway to make a point to Riley, she'd morphed into a stage-five clinger. In front of Riley, I was fine with that, but without her around, it wasn't serving much purpose.

There was another way I could get under Riley's skin. I took Eliana's hand and pulled her off the couch and behind me. She jogged to keep up with my long strides. I found a playlist on my phone when I got to my room and turned the volume up— anything to annoy Riley.

After five minutes, she still hadn't come out to yell. Eliana pressed herself against me. I turned my head when she linked her hands around my neck, went onto her toes, and tried to kiss me. I couldn't take my eyes off the door. *Any minute now.* Riley had a temper. The loud music and Eliana being in the house had to trigger her.

It seemed like Eliana had eight arms with how much she kept touching me, and I batted her away. It was like being caught in a spider's web. Overpowering floral perfume enveloped me in a headache-inducing cloud. And it smelled vaguely familiar. "Are you wearing the perfume Piper wears?"

"Yeah," She flashed a coy smile then backed up. "I thought you would like it."

"Not particularly." I preferred the lilac-and-honey scent that clung to Riley's skin.

"Well, maybe you'll like this better." She grabbed the hem of her form-fitting shirt then whipped it off. She advanced in a lacy white bra just as my door slammed open so hard that it bounced off the wall.

Perfect timing.

"Turn the music down!" Riley stomped to my dresser, still with the towel wrapped around her swimsuit-clad body, grabbed my phone, and hit the button to pause the music. Then she turned to me, spotting Eliana wearing only her bra. The fight left Riley's face, and her expression shuttered. Anything else she might've said died as she handed me the phone. She walked out, slamming the door behind her.

I hated it. I wanted to know what she was thinking and feeling. When she put that wall back in place, it left me feeling cold.

"What's she doing here?" Eliana frowned.

She hadn't seen Riley downstairs because her back had been to the patio door. But she was full of shit. Miss Gossip Queen knew why Riley was living here. I'd had enough.

"Time to go." I ushered a protesting, shirt-clutching, half-naked girl downstairs and out the door. Once she was clear, I shut and locked it.

I could admit to myself why I'd let Eliana in—I'd wanted to make Riley as insanely jealous as I'd been when Jarrett touched her shoulder at lunch, and she hadn't done a damn thing to stop him.

The need to argue with Riley propelled me up the stairs and to her door. I banged on the wood then shoved it open as she came out of the bathroom, wearing a black bra and panties. *Goddamn.* Never in all my life had I seen a sexier sight.

I couldn't say anything, so I reacted. Two steps, and I was in front of her, pulling her into my arms. I shuddered from the feel of her body pressed to mine. I buried one hand in her thick dark hair, the other secure at the small of her back, keeping her where I wanted her.

I'd had a half-naked girl in my room a while ago but had felt nothing. All I would have had to do was kiss Eliana, and she would've fallen into bed with me.

With Riley—I feel everything.

I dropped my face to her neck and inhaled. She was like a drug. An electrical current passed through me, heating my blood even more. I hungered for her. I had to know if she was equally affected and if the thought of me with anyone else also drove her mad. "Were you jealous?"

She shuddered, and I grinned against the softness of her skin. "No." Her voice was raspy, tormented. "I'm only sorry I slept with you in the first place."

Bullshit. I tugged at a fistful of hair at the nape of her neck, not too hard but enough to make her arch into me. She was just as affected as I was. With a gentle nip at her neck, I told her how it was. "You belong to me. Even if you deny it with words, your body says otherwise."

"I don't belong to anyone"—hands flat on my chest, she shoved—"especially someone who had another girl in his arms a few minutes ago."

She pushed at me again. I released her hair and caught her wrists, pinning them behind her back before my mouth slanted over hers. She struggled. I tightened my hold, backing her against the wall before deepening the kiss, exploring and taking my time. Desire raged through my body. When she moaned, I growled into her mouth, releasing her hands.

Free, she explored under my shirt, her fingertips tracing my abs. Everywhere she touched, I burned with need. I wanted to sink into her warmth more than I needed my next breath.

She sucked in my bottom lip, and I groaned. The girl drove me crazy. Then her hands were in my hair, her nails scraping lightly against my scalp. Then she gave a sharp tug, breaking our kiss.

A rush of raw need flooded my system as I stared into her

passion-darkened eyes. The thing was, her actions only made me hotter. I would never get enough.

I brushed the pad of my thumb across her kiss-swollen bottom lip before tucking a long strand of hair behind her ear then releasing her. I stepped back to the door, where I paused and leveled her with a heated look. "This isn't over."

I've got her right where I want her.

CHAPTER EIGHTEEN

RILEY

He's an asshole. But holy hell, can he kiss.

For the tenth time, I brushed my fingers across my lips, which still tingled from yesterday's encounter with the jerk. Trapped in the same house, I barricaded myself in my room, reading a romance novel I'd swiped from their library. It was all I could do to stop myself from jumping him. Because that kiss played on repeat, heating my body to unbearable temperatures.

I hate him, but I want him. It never ended.

With two days left of suspension, nothing to do, and the knowledge that Cole was in the house, I sat and watched the rain pelt my window. Every once in a while, a flash of lightning would tear across the sky, followed by a boom of thunder. I tossed the book onto my bed, having read the same paragraph twice and still having no idea what it said. My stomach growled for the tenth time as a knock sounded on my door.

"I ordered a pizza if you want to share."

"I don't." *Good thing he didn't open the door.* I wasn't sure how I would've reacted. I eyed the cover of the romance novel. It might have been a bad choice since I was already heated.

I grabbed my phone and watched mindless videos. Another half hour passed until I couldn't ignore how hungry I was. I dropped my phone onto the bed next to the book and tiptoed out of my room, stopping in front of his door. I pressed my ear against it and listened for any sign that he was inside. Hard to tell. The heavy rain was noisy.

My stomach growled again, and I cringed, swiftly backing away from the door. I took care to avoid the steps that squeaked on my way down. Once in the kitchen, I caught the faint sound of the TV. Cole's eyes went from the screen to his phone and back again.

I pressed my lips into a tight line, annoyed by his presence. He didn't have to be there. If his brother or cousins weren't in school or football practice, he would have been with them. Things in the house weren't fair. I wasn't allowed to go anywhere. If Mom had delivered that mandate, I could have accepted it, but Lucas had thought he had the right to boss me around before the two had left for some client thing.

I got it. I did. If Nick was closing in on us, I shouldn't have been running around where he might spot me. I wasn't stupid. It wasn't my first brush with my dad being in the same town.

Mom still hadn't said a thing. I was beyond pissed. We needed to talk whenever she returned to the house that was *not* our home despite how much she pretended it was.

I gritted my teeth as I opened the fridge to see what there was to eat. I was all kinds of worked up from the constant memory of Cole's kiss, the romance novel, and being stuck with him in such close proximity.

After scanning the shelves for the pizza, I turned. He was right behind me. I tilted my head back to give him the full power of my scowl. "You need to wear a bell so people know when you're coming and can get out of the way."

Green eyes flashed in amusement as he crowded me even more. "You're not in my way."

I crossed my arms over my chest and leaned back into the cold shelving to maintain an inch of space between us. "Wonder what your little girlfriend would think of you rubbing against me." Without taking my eyes off him and that sexy smirk, I flailed behind me until my hand rested on something round. I latched onto it and slipped past him, flustered that I'd grabbed an apple instead of the pizza I wanted.

I went back into my room, ate the apple, and picked the book back up to read. There was no way I was going back down there. With something in my stomach, I could focus on the story. The book was pretty good. I read a few chapters, not even noticing my door was open until the sound of glass clinked.

My eyes flew to where he stood in my doorway, a bottle of whiskey in one hand and two glasses in the other. *Interesting.* I was intrigued.

"You may enter." I cracked myself up. I was in a weird mood. I blamed the book.

His deep laugh sent shivers over my body. I was too aware of him.

"Damon is going to Phoenix's after school, and our parents are in LA." He splashed amber liquid into one glass, handed it to me, then poured one for him. "I thought that since we have to be stuck in the house together, we should call a truce."

I narrowed my eyes. It was a trap. I wasn't born yesterday, but I was going stir-crazy. So… what the hell. I was game, even if it was the middle of the afternoon. "Okay."

He sat on my bed, picked up the book, and opened to the last page I'd read. He skimmed the print before setting the book on my nightstand and taking a drink.

I couldn't help but wonder if it got him hot. I was already revved up from him kissing me last night, and I wanted him to get ideas—not that he needed help. *God, just looking at him makes me melt.*

I took a sip, letting the alcohol burn a path down my throat.

I wasn't a big drinker. One would probably be it for me. It wasn't worth the risk to consume more than that, especially with things on such high alert. *It never pays to lose your instincts or ability to run.*

It was weird as fuck that Mom wasn't around. Very unlike her. I snapped out of my head when I realized Cole was watching me over the rim of his glass as he took a sip.

"What's going on in that head of yours? I can practically hear the gears turning."

"Just wondering if that book made you hot." I felt myself blush, having blurted out the first thing that came to mind. I was usually much quicker on my feet, but I'd been off for the past two days.

He set his drink down, took mine from me, and put it next to his. His features turned predatory, and desire swirled in his eyes. "I don't need a book to make me hot." He cupped the back of my neck, applying gentle pressure. "All I need is you."

God, when he says those things... Anticipation skated across my skin, and I curled my fingers into the soft duvet. I wanted him so badly and gave in to the tug to come closer. I rested my hands on his shoulders, and he dropped his to my waist, lifting me. I willingly straddled him. Then his mouth was on mine, and nothing else mattered but how he made me feel.

He took control of the kiss, teasing until I parted for him. I moaned as he sank his teeth into my bottom lip. His tongue darted out, running over the tender spot before he slanted his mouth over mine in a drugging kiss that I swore I felt in my soul.

I explored the corded muscles of his neck, shoulders, and along his back, pressing myself as close as I could. His fingers slipped beneath the hem of my shirt, and I eased back enough for him to slip it over my head. My bra was soon to follow. I tugged at his shirt, craving the sensation of his skin on mine.

But for a moment, I just stared. He let me because he was

doing the same. I wasn't even embarrassed because all I could process was how sinfully beautiful he was. A work of art. A human replica of one of the Greek gods. And for tonight, he was mine.

I sank my fingers into his thick black hair and tugged as he devoured me. His hands went to my hips, and he rocked me against him. I squirmed, reveling in his hardness, dizzy with want. He trailed up my back with a featherlight touch then buried his fingers in the hair at my nape. He gave a gentle tug, and I arched, exposing my neck to him.

Soft kisses trailed down my neck, stopping where my pulse fluttered against my skin. The sensation of his lips on my body drove me crazy. The scrape of his teeth, a sharp bite, and another open-mouthed kiss sent shocks of need to my core.

He commanded my body, and I let him.

He traced the undersides of my breasts with gentle fingers. I ached for him. My body swelled and plumped, my nipples screaming for his touch. He took one in his mouth, and I moaned as heat pooled low, my core a tight ball of need. I gripped his shoulders and felt the muscles bunching and rippling beneath my fingers.

Without warning, he stood. I gasped and clung to him, my legs automatically wrapping around his waist. One finger moved between us, and he slipped it between the waistband of my small sleep shorts, urging them down as my legs slid down his body. There was too much space between us. I forced myself to remain still, just barely, as he stepped out of the rest of his clothes.

Desire tore through me. He was mouthwatering. There were so many things I wanted to do to him. I reached for his hard length, but he only chuckled and brushed my hand away, the deep cadence of his laugh teasing my senses. I wanted to touch and lick him everywhere, making him lose control.

His hands gripped my waist and moved me effortlessly

where he wanted me. I lay on the bed, my hands moving over him while he explored my body. With every touch, electricity sizzled along my skin. I was past the point of fighting the addiction.

Needing greater access, I curled into a sitting position, and he lifted me back into his lap. My hand brushed the side of his arousal. When he groaned, a jolt of power shot through me, and I curled my fingers around him.

He gave a sharp intake of breath then caught my eye and shook his head, his features tight with tense need and desire dilating his pupils. I pouted for a second before he distracted me with the pad of his finger against my clit. He made slows circles with gentle pressure, and I sucked my lower lip between my teeth, unsuccessfully stifling a wanton moan.

He spread me wide, bare to his view. The moment's vulnerability teased the edges of my mind, but I was too far gone. I shivered in anticipation at the gleam in his eyes. Then he flipped me around, my back to his chest. Legs bent, my ass pressed against his length, and I stiffened.

"N—"

"Relax," he crooned near my ear while his fingers bit into my hip and his other hand tangled in my hair, holding me still. "I'm not doing anything you don't want. We'll save that for another time."

He chuckled at my gasp. *Like hell we will.* Some dark part of me, though, wondered what it would be like if he went in the back door. He breathed harder, and I glanced up. Holy hell— he'd positioned us so he could watch us in the mirror over my dresser. It was erotic. Sexy. And I was shocked by how much I liked it.

He released me for a brief moment, rolled a condom on, then eased me back against him. My body protested, not wanting to give him entry. Soft kisses trailed along my spine, and his hands caressed my breasts until I relaxed. He held still when he was fully seated in me, giving me time to adjust.

One hand slid around to my stomach to dip between my legs. The pads of his fingers spread me wide then teased around where he was inside me, coating my clit with slickness. I could feel myself plump beneath his touch. The more he touched me, the wetter I got. As he increased the friction, I clenched around him. I pushed back, desperate for more, but his hand held me in place.

He was so large everywhere, corded muscles straining against tight skin. His size made me feel small and delicate.

I arched my back and pressed my shoulders against his chest as he wrapped my long hair around his fist and held me tight.

Then he moved my hips, slowly at first then faster. I felt him everywhere. Jolts of desire shot through my body, and I panted. He made a noise that was half groan and half growl behind me then released my hair and pulled me off him. I was flat on my back, and he rose over me. My body quivered with need as he lined up then thrust deeply.

A moan ripped through my body at the burst of sensations. He increased the pace, and my nails dug into his shoulders, my legs wrapping around him as I matched his rhythm.

I writhed beneath him as he hit that magical spot. My body reacted. His mouth descended on mine just as explosions rocked my body and I went over the edge. Stars burst behind my eyelids, and he swallowed my scream. Two thrusts, and he followed me with his own orgasm.

His weight settled over me, and I welcomed it, running my fingertips up and down his back as we caught our breath. My body was so relaxed that it felt boneless—I didn't want to move. Cole shifted then pulled out, and I instantly felt the loss. When he got up, goose bumps raced over my skin. He took care of the condom then returned to bed and gathered me in his arms.

Exhausted, I rested my head on his chest, content and safe. I was on the cusp of sleep, but I couldn't help but think of how he made me want things I couldn't have.

How the hell will I let him go?

CHAPTER NINETEEN

COLE

Each time with Riley is better than the last.

I didn't mean to have sex with her again. Okay, I did. But I didn't mean to fall asleep in her room. And I must have slept for a few hours because it was pitch-black outside when I awoke.

I lay in her bed, enjoying the feeling of her pressed against me. There was no way I was going back to mine.

Rain pounded like angry little fists against the windowpanes. Lightning strobed through her room, and thunder boomed so loudly that I swore the picture on her dresser rattled. It caught my eye, and I eased from beneath the covers. Careful not to make a sound, I lifted the picture and studied the image of Riley and Raelyn at a beach. Curious, I opened the frame to see if any others were behind it. Instead of encountering the smooth back of a print, there was a piece of folded paper. *Interesting.*

I put the frame back together, set it down, then shoved the note into my pants on the ground before returning to bed. More pressing things were at hand—specifically being in bed with Riley.

The air felt electric. I glanced at the clock, but the glowing numbers were dark. The power must have gone out, no surprise given the storm directly overhead and how close the crack of thunder had followed the strobing lightning.

As the lightning shot silvery beams across the bed, I visually traced what she looked like asleep. Soft and sexy, her lashes fanned across high cheekbones. Full lips parted slightly. She breathed deeply. Beneath her eyelids, her eyes moved rapidly. A deafening crack of thunder caused her body to jerk, and she flinched, burrowing closer to me.

Her breathing quickened, and I ran my hand up and down her back, trying to calm her. It didn't help. At the next clap of thunder, her eyes popped open wide with panic.

"It's okay, Riles. Just a storm." I recognized the level of panic from the time she woke with a nightmare and wanted me to stay with her. "Want to talk about it?"

She shook her head.

I pushed because I was concerned. "We called a truce, remember? I promise not to use what you tell me against you." I meant it. There was something very wrong, and I didn't want to mess with her anymore.

I didn't push. I just waited. The darkness helped. I felt myself wanting to share too. And I would, but only after she did. I felt like I was bouncing from one extreme to the other—how I felt about her, all the mess surrounding Mom's death… Underneath all of that, what mattered was *Riley* and how much I liked her for the strong and very talented person she was. She was a survivor, and I respected the hell out of her for it.

"A storm like this one came through one night long ago. I swear it was an omen. I felt the warning but didn't say anything to Mom. My silence almost came at the price of her life."

My arms tightened around her as I sensed her slipping into the memory. I knew all about those and didn't want her to go alone. But I kept silent, wanting her to confide in me so I could share the burden.

"It was the night before he found us. Mom's ex. My father." She pushed out a humorless laugh. "If he can be called that. He's not a good guy." Dark emotion filled her words, raising the hairs on the back of my neck and making me pay close attention to what she said and what she didn't. "Following the night of the storm, he found Mom. Beat her and knocked her out cold. When she didn't come home when she said she would, I went after her. It was a miracle he hadn't taken her phone. I found her... with help. We got her out of there and went on the run again. Like always. We're always running."

I didn't think it was a mistake that her father had left Raelyn's phone on her. Nor did I believe Riley thought so, either. It was a way for Riley to track her mom and for her dad to lure her to him.

"Why did he beat her up?" I couldn't help but wonder if she'd cheated on him, and I barely stopped myself from saying it. But we were in a truce, and I was committed to not being an asshole for the next few days. Lightning flashed, and I caught her glare.

"Whatever you're thinking about my mom, it's wrong. My father is a terrible person. Dangerous. And her leaving him was the only way to save us both."

"That's what the nightmare was about that one night? Finding your mom like that?" A shiver tore through her, and I went back to running my hand up and down her back.

"Yeah." Her voice was unusually small. "It was horrifying. And I know that she would have been much worse off if he hadn't left for whatever had called him away."

My PI hadn't uncovered who her father was, not yet. But the pieces of her life fell into place. "The cons? What's that about? And is my father one of them?" Part of me didn't care if he was, but I had to know. The real question I wanted to ask was whether I was too.

"It was how we survived. A job is traceable. Even with..."

"A different name?"

She sighed. "Yeah. Taking a job at the Coffee Cabana over the summer wasn't smart, but I was angry at Mom because she said she had a boyfriend here, and I needed something to do."

It was as close to a confession as I'd gotten. "Wasn't that what she did for cons, get a guy on the hook?" I knew they did other scams. Wes told me about one. And if she'd worked for Dad back then, he must have been a mark.

"No, not really. We would do personal assistant jobs and hit up petty cash for the most part, which was why we never had a ton of money. Scamming a guy by pretending to be engaged was a huge risk, and Mom and I agreed it wasn't worth our safety or sanity." She gripped my bicep in a tight squeeze. "Don't think you can use that against us by going to the cops. I've got way too much on you too."

Underground fighting. Yeah, she does. "I wasn't." I meant it. That wasn't what I did. My brother and cousins solved things our way. There was no need for legal intervention.

"Our parents knew each other when we were little. My mom loves your dad. She told me he's the only man she's ever felt that way about, but she had to run the first time they met. She ghosted him. There was no other way. I guess he never stopped searching for her. He found us last year, so we moved back."

"Do you believe her?" Anger speared me. "Because I sure as shit don't think he's capable of loving Raelyn the way you describe."

"I do. She's never stayed before. We should have left already. It's not smart. But she has this unwavering trust that your dad can do something to help us. And then there's the way she looks at him. I've never seen her let her guard down with anyone before. There are rules."

I chuckled. She sounded so outraged. "What rules?"

She leaned back slightly and then ticked them off her fingers. "No social media. Don't stand out. Blend in. Never get emotionally involved. And never tell anyone where we came from. Or worse, who we're running from."

"And she told my dad."

"Yep." She popped the "p."

I didn't point out that she'd broken those rules too. The meet where she did that dive that brought the crowd to their feet… news traveled fast. Even though I wasn't there, I'd heard about it. The article Skylar did in the school paper had listed her by her last name only—Matthews.

But she'd confided in me about her dad, the cons, the running. And it softened me more toward her.

We fell silent for several minutes. Wind howled outside the window, throwing rain harder at the glass panes. As I lay in bed with Riley in my arms, I realized I'd never felt so close to another person. I found myself wanting to confide in her too. "That book you were reading was my mom's. She used to love romance novels. Damon and I would pick them up for her. Completely embarrassing." I laughed at the memory, and it felt good.

"Oh." She covered her face with her hands. "No wonder reading that page didn't make you hot. Who wouldn't be weirded out by that?"

My body shook with laughter. "Yeah, there's that." Then I sobered because there was more that she had to know. "Last year, my mom asked Damon and me to go to the legal conference Dad was at. She had strict instructions for us to hand deliver a note and not to leave until he read it. Your mom was there."

"I figured out that it was your dad who brought us here when we came back. I'm sorry. Mom told me he was married but that he was leaving her."

I snorted. Everything he'd done came back in a tidal wave of hatred. "After Dad read the letter, he ran out of the conference. Damon and I did the same. We never saw what the note said, but for him to react that way... we knew she'd told him something terrifying.

"She knew he was cheating on her, and she'd put up with him humiliating her for too long. It affected her deeply and caused bouts of depression. When we got home, he tried to stop us from entering their room. I shoved him, and Damon got in first. Then I did. I'll never forget that moment. Mom was lying on her bed, surrounded by empty pill bottles. Her eyes were open but sightless. We couldn't save her." A shudder shook me, and I swallowed the howl of pain that wanted to come out. I could still see her lifeless body. All the old emotions from that day converged in an overwhelming rush.

Riley cupped the side of my face. "I'm so sorry, Cole." Her words were soft and heartfelt.

I jerked back. If she kept touching me, I would fall apart, and there was no way I would let myself go there. I rolled to the edge of the bed and stood. I found my shorts, put them on, and then rushed out of her room. I needed a minute to get it together, to push the painful memories away.

It wasn't her fault and maybe not even Raelyn's—it was my dad's. *Fuck.* I scrubbed my hands over my face before going downstairs. When I got to the first floor, the sound of rain was overly loud. Wind whipped through with a chilling burst. That's when I noticed the door was wide open. I stepped on a palm frond and frowned. *Did I forget to lock it after the pizza delivery?*

That has to be it. Either that or the battery backup didn't kick in when the wind blew the door open. Perfect. I shut and locked the door then turned to go into the kitchen to get some paper towels and a mop.

I didn't get far. A dark figure appeared, and I tensed, ready to fight as lightning flashed, illuminating the person and showing me that it wasn't anyone I knew.

"You must be the boy who's fucking my whore daughter."

CHAPTER TWENTY

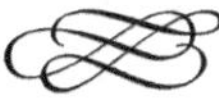

RILEY

I should go after Cole. But I won't.

I flopped onto my back, warring with myself over what to do. *His mom killed herself. It was horrible. He found her.* I couldn't even imagine. Tears misted my eyes, and I furiously blinked them away.

He'd slammed out of my room with such conviction—he sure as hell needed space. And I understood, but I couldn't let him be alone, no matter how much I thought I should. We'd shared too much tonight, both physically and mentally. I got out of bed and pulled on my sleep shorts and a T-shirt.

I opened the door and shivered. It was oddly chilly in the house. I went down the hall to the top of the landing but paused. I heard voices. The hairs on the back of my neck stood at attention. *Angry voices.*

Did Lucas come back early? Are he and Cole arguing?

I took a few cautious steps down the stairs. Then I heard the sound of a fist hitting flesh. It couldn't have been Lucas. He might have been an asshole, but I couldn't see him hitting his kid.

"If you touch her, I'll kill you." Cole's voice held so much venom that my hand shook on the railing as I raced to the first floor.

"You'll be dead before you can try." Another succession of punches sounded. "Stay down, punk."

Bile climbed my throat, and I stopped in my tracks. I knew that voice, and he was close. I'd only heard it one other time. I had to get to a phone. It was the only way to save both of us. Because even if he took me, Cole would need help. I wouldn't go there, imagining what my dad had already done to him. Pushing through the fear, I took off.

There was a landline in Lucas's study. If I could make it there, I could call for help. I ran to his study, grabbed the phone, and pressed it to my ear. My hands hovered over the buttons, but there was no dial tone. *Fuck.* He probably used a cable service, and the line was dead due to the storm.

"Riley."

White-hot fear shot through me, and I dropped the receiver, grabbed the first thing I saw on the desk, then raced around and hid under it. I didn't dare pull the chair any closer in case it made noise or he was close enough to see it move.

I wrapped my arms around my knees, huddling in the back corner and trying to make myself as small as possible. The only good thing about the power being out was that he couldn't turn on a light.

What I wouldn't give for a long metal letter opener. But I'd grabbed a pen. I could work with that, but it wouldn't be nearly as effective. Carefully, I removed the cap during one of the claps of thunder.

Every second felt like an hour, and every sound was loud as a bomb. My nerves were shredded. I couldn't even think about what he'd done to Cole, or I would lose it. The whole thing was so stupid. If only my uncle had been there, we would have stood a chance. But with only Cole and me... *Oh God, we aren't going to make it.*

How did he find us?

The fucking storm and bad omens. I should have listened to that feeling, same as that time before. But in bed with Cole, I'd been distracted. *Now, we're going to die.*

I mentally slapped myself. *I'm stronger than that.* I took a deep breath and held it for a moment before releasing it just as slowly. A sense of control returned along with the ability to think. I calculated what would happen.

He would find me. It was inevitable. I gripped the pen in my fist. I'd watched *Bourne Identity* many times. I knew how to wield a pen. When that asshole pulled me out from under the desk, I would be ready.

In small quiet movements, I turned so my left arm was facing the opening. I needed to have the full range of my right.

The door burst open and bounced off the wall with a *thud*. I rolled the pen back in my fingers and tightened the grip, bracing for what would happen next. The chair launched back from the desk, and a small penlight was in my face. I tucked my fist close to my chest.

A meaty hand curled around my arm, and he dragged me out. I could barely see in the dark room after that LED light flashed in my eyes. I was yanked to my feet and held tightly to him. It didn't matter. I had the outline of where I had to strike. I swung with all my might and sank the pen into his neck.

I wanted to feel the spurt of blood. If I had, that meant I'd hit an artery. Then there would be approximately thirty seconds until he bled out.

He cursed and then threw me across the room. I landed hard on my back. I couldn't breathe. Short gasps were all I could manage, not enough to get the air into my lungs. My brain screamed along with my straining lungs. I couldn't panic. He'd just knocked the wind out of me. *I'm fine.* I relaxed as much as I could, waiting it out.

I took a full breath then sprang into action. I scrambled to my knees, but he was on me. He wore a suit and stunk of cigar smoke. Pain exploded along my scalp when he fisted my hair, yanking me back. I frantically grabbed his wrist, trying to alleviate the pressure on the roots as he dragged me by my hair from the room and down the hall.

Tears stung my eyes and trickled down my face. I tried to get my legs under me, but we were going too fast, and all I could do was hold onto his wrist. He let go and shoved me to the floor in in the foyer, next to Cole, who wasn't moving.

Is he dead? I shook as I reached out to touch him.

"Don't move."

"Fuck you!" I needed to know. I pressed my fingers against Cole's neck, frantically feeling for a pulse. I felt it beat against the pads of my fingers and sagged back in relief.

Nick—there was no way I was referring to him as "Dad" even in my head—kicked at my foot, and I pulled my legs up. Then I noticed the gun. I scrambled to the right and angled my body to block as much of Cole as possible.

The gun stayed steady as he tossed a phone at me. I caught it out of reflex.

"Call your mother. Tell her Daddy's home." His tone was mocking and cold.

"Gross. I just threw up in my mouth." The flash of lightning gave me a frightening glimpse of his lack of amusement. I didn't care. He was disgusting, and it was much easier to fall into sarcasm than to allow the fear to take hold again.

But one good thing came from the added light. I saw the trail of blood on the side of his neck from where I'd punctured the skin with the pen. Good. I hoped it hurt like hell. And we looked nothing alike. I was never happier to look like a carbon copy of Mom. I wanted nothing notably genetic from the killer threatening me.

I angled the phone so he couldn't see and pressed 911 but faked hitting a few more numbers as if I was calling Mom. *He must think I'm an idiot—he didn't make me put the call on speaker. Guess he's the idiot.*

There was no way I would call Mom. He would kill her. So I guessed he would have to kill me instead. The operator answered, and I infused as much fear in my voice as I could. It wasn't hard. I was scared out of my mind.

"Mom," I said over the operator, "Dad's here. He has a gun. He wants you to come home right away." I waited for a beat as if she'd said something. "No, I'm not at the rental. I came back to the Savages' place on Riverhill Drive. Hurry, Mom. He hurt Cole." I hung up but didn't hand the phone back until he held out his hand for it.

I tossed it, not wanting to touch him. He pressed a button on his phone then advanced. I cringed back, not knowing what he would do. Then pain exploded across my face with his back-hand slap. I fell to my side, my head whipping back from the force of his hit. As he straightened, pointing the gun at Cole, I screamed.

Cole launched himself from a prone position so quickly that I could barely track him. He plowed into Nick, and the gun went off with an ear-ringing blast. Something shattered. They went down. Cole knocked the weapon away. It clattered across the marble floor, and I jumped to my feet and dashed for it.

They rolled around, punching each other. One second Cole had the upper hand, then Nick. My fingers curled around the gun. The heavy weight felt right in my hand, and everything in me settled.

"Stop!" I screamed at them. When they didn't listen, I aimed at the ceiling and squeezed the trigger. Water rained down on us. I must have hit a pipe. I didn't care. All that mattered was ending this.

Cole stood over Nick. He moved to the left when he saw what I held, so I had a clear shot. I aimed as red-and-blue lights flashed through the windows. The door burst open.

My hand never wavered as I pointed the barrel at Nick. It would have been so easy to shoot. I wouldn't have to worry about looking over my shoulder again. Mom would be safe. We wouldn't have to move all the time.

I didn't want the cops there. I could hear them talking to me as if I was underwater. They were telling me to be calm, to put the gun down. But if I didn't shoot, it would never end. *He'll never stop coming for us. It's the only way to be safe.*

Cole was at my side. The heat of his body radiated into my chilled flesh. His hand slid down my arm to the gun in a soothing caress, and I whimpered at how gentle it was. "Let go, Riley. I'll make sure you're safe."

"But I won't be." *Doesn't he see? It's the only way.*

"You'll go to jail." His lips were at my ear, whispering, "And I don't want to lose you like that."

He took the gun.

It was over.

For now.

CHAPTER TWENTY-ONE

COLE

I was furious. At my dad. At Riley's mom. At that motherfucker who'd broken into the house. At the goddammed concussion from that asshole, Nick Viareggio, pistol-whipping me with the butt of his gun. The head injury, though mild, would keep me out of practice and games for the next few weeks. I'd learned his name when the cops arrived.

But most of all, rage simmered inside me at the danger Riley had been in.

The rain had stopped, but clouds remained. Humidity hung in the air as densely as everyone's lousy mood in the car. It was Thursday morning, and we were on our way home from the hospital, where Riley and I had gotten checked out. Dad and a very shaken Raelyn were in the front seat. No one spoke.

It was eerie as hell. Riley sat beside me, tightly clenching her hands in her lap, staring straight ahead. She'd answered questions from the police and the doctor, but she hadn't said much else. I didn't like it. Something was going on, and I suspected it went beyond the incident with Nick.

The doctors had checked her and found her uninjured aside from the bruise on her cheek from Nick's backhand, but when she looked at me or anyone else, it was like she didn't see anything.

Dad pulled into the driveway behind our cousins' and Damon's SUVs. I wasn't surprised to see them there rather than in school. Dad wasn't, either, given his unchanged expression. We got out of the car, and Raelyn hung back until Riley moved to her side. She clung to Riley's arm as they went inside then straight upstairs.

Dad stopped at the entrance, surveying the damage. "Thanks for cleaning everything up. Is Louisa inside?"

"No." Damon leaned the broom against the wall. "I thought you might want her to have paid time off with everything going on. I called her and said you would follow up when you're home later."

I stepped past Dad, remaining quiet to see what he and everyone else would do. He must have called Damon. I hadn't had a chance, and I knew I would catch hell from my brother later. My gaze strayed to a blank space on the wall just off the foyer, where one of our large family pictures had hung, and remembered the sound of the gun going off when I'd tackled Nick. The family portrait was gone, and there was a bullet hole in the wall where it had hung.

"The water's still off," Damon informed us.

At least the power was on.

"I called a plumber. He'll be here this afternoon," Phoenix said as Shane took the broom and dustpan from Damon into the kitchen.

"I have some calls to make." Dad turned to me. "Take it easy. You know the drill: no screens, bright lights, or loud music. I'm going to work from home for the next week. Let me know if you need something or aren't feeling well."

Is it the concussion, or are they all strange? Damon wasn't throwing attitude. My dad was being reasonable. Phoenix and Shane were super quiet, Riley was in shock, and her mom was terrified. I needed a calm, dark place where I could talk to Damon and our cousins. *Basement.*

I headed there. They followed.

We sat on the couch, then the questions started. I held up a hand, the pain in my head making it tough to listen. I filled them in on what had happened, but they knew most of it.

"Dad called and got us out of school and home," Damon said. "He hired security for us and Aunt Cece, just in case."

"He doesn't think Riley's dad will stay in prison." Phoenix confirmed my fear.

I wasn't surprised that Dad hadn't told us. He was trying to protect Riley and her mom and keep them from panicking. But something told me they knew.

"I'm glad you stayed at their house last night," I said to Damon. He'd texted that they were having a video game marathon, and he didn't feel like driving home from Phoenix and Shane's. I hadn't thought anything of it at the time. But if he had been home, I could have lost him. There had been a fucking gun… It bothered me more than I cared to admit. I'd already lost Mom. I couldn't lose my brother too. *And I can't lose Riley.*

We shared a look, and I saw my own thoughts and feelings reflected in Damon's eyes. That'd been too close for comfort. "Dad called you and fill you in on what happened?"

"Yeah. He wanted the three of us to come straight home from practice, but we left after his call. It wasn't long after we got here that the cops took off and security arrived."

I stood. "You guys staying?"

"We are." Phoenix's features were granite, a sign that he hated what was happening. We needed to strategize, but not at the moment. "Mom's working tonight, and your dad has security on her when she leaves the hospital."

"Okay." I headed for the stairs. "I'm crashing. Wake me if anything happens"—I paused on the first step—"or for dinner."

Dad was in his office and on the phone when I got to the

first floor. We made brief eye contact, and I read the worry there. Riley's door was closed on the second floor, and I could make out the faint sound of her Mom's voice. Exhausted, I made sure my blinds were closed, shut the door, and got into bed. It didn't take long for my body to shut down. I passed out.

***

In the middle of the night, I couldn't sleep with Riley so close but so far away. I shoved off the covers and slipped from my room and into hers, closing the door behind me. She lay on the bed, unmoving and barely blinking. She didn't even look at me when I came in.

Her room was dark, except for the light of the moon. Quiet. And she still wasn't speaking.

I sat on the bed beside her, curling my fingers around hers. "When my mom died, I couldn't get the image of her lying there out of my head. I know it's not the same as what happened with Nick"—I wouldn't call him her father—"but I didn't want to talk to anybody, either."

When her hand tightened around mine, I lay beside her, waiting until her eyelids drifted closed. Only then did I relax enough to fall asleep, knowing I wouldn't let anyone get to her.

CHAPTER TWENTY-TWO

RILEY

I couldn't sleep, even with Cole beside me. Aside from the time Nick had caught and beaten Mom, I'd never been so scared.

Not of him or what he'd done to Cole. I was afraid of myself and what I wanted to do—would have done if Cole hadn't stopped me. I would have killed my father, which meant that part of me was like him. I would have shot him without hesitation. A chill raced over my arms. *I came so close.* I didn't know how to come to terms with it.

Right as the first light of dawn peeked through my blinds, as Cole breathed deeply and evenly beside me, I slipped out of bed and changed. In jail, Nick wasn't a concern, but he would be. Mom and I knew he would be free sooner rather than later. He had too many lawyers and too many people in his pocket to be kept behind bars.

I had to go somewhere. A slight sound from the door opening and closing was the only noise I made leaving my room. I stood on the other side of the door in the hallway, listening for movement. When I heard nothing, I crept down the stairs and to the alarm panel. I shut it off then reset it, using the time delay to go outside. My car was in the driveway. Within minutes, I was behind the wheel and heading for the cove.

The storm was long gone, a distant bad memory, and I took the mild weather as a sign of peace and safety. I made the drive on autopilot, parked, then got out and found the steep and rocky path. I climbed to one of the higher jumping spots I'd said I would do someday. That day had come. I needed it.

I held still, watching the rippling water below. I craved the exhilaration and freedom of diving from a height that rivaled Olympic high dives. I knew it was a foolish risk, especially from that point on the cliff. If I didn't twist enough or landed wrong, I could break my neck or back.

Various moments had burned themselves like brands into my psyche. I had too many scars. I tried to replace the stain of the most recent by grounding myself in the high spot, focusing on the warmth of the wind caressing my skin and brushing my hair off my face. The scent of wildflowers, dirt, and water. The sound of a pebble rolling down the rocks off to my right, probably disturbed by a small critter. The utter peacefulness of the place.

Time felt suspended. I should have envisioned the dive, but all I could do was relive the night before and what could have been—what I could have done. A flash of headlights caught my notice as a car pulled into the small parking lot below. The driver's side door opened. Cole stepped out then looked up.

I didn't move. Since he'd taken the gun from my hand, a numbness had stolen over me and had yet to dissipate. I waited for him to climb the path.

It wasn't long before he stood a foot behind me. My skin prickled with awareness, and a spark of life flared somewhere deep inside of me. If he touched me, the numbness would retreat.

Do I want that? I wasn't sure.

"Did you follow me?" I continued to look ahead, staring sightlessly over the cove. He stayed slightly behind me, probably sensing my unstable mood. After surviving his mother's death by suicide, I knew he understood.

His hatred for Mom and me made sense once he'd explained the events that led to her leaving them. I would have done worse, so I couldn't blame him.

"Kind of."

I had to think for a moment before remembering I'd asked if he'd followed me.

"Your Mom's worried. I said I would find you. I checked the school first."

Right, because of the pool. I had gone there in the past. Today was different. I couldn't turn around, not yet. Feeling his strength was enough. One look at those knowing eyes or that stunning face, and I would cave. I needed this dive.

"Are you going to dive? Or are you jumping for another reason?"

I nodded then paused. "I want to dive, but not yet. I'm here to think." *Not to talk.*

"Okay."

He moved back, but it didn't matter. I would always feel his presence. I stepped away from the edge and faced him. I wasn't prepared. The sun crested the horizon and caught the gold flecks in his green eyes. I wanted to run my fingers through his dark hair and feel the safety of his arms as they wound around me. The numbness faded, as I knew it would.

He'd fought for me, and I owed him so much. "Thank you for saving me yesterday." My voice cracked. There was no help for how choked up I was.

"You're the one who saved me."

A laugh escaped, surprising me, and I relaxed a tiny bit. That wasn't true, and we both knew it, but I appreciated him making light of the situation, allowing me to breathe easier. "I would have killed him. If you hadn't stopped me..."

A bird's cry sounded overhead, and I took another step closer to him as if an invisible cord connected us. "How are you feeling?" The doctor had said he had a mild concussion, thanks to Nick hitting him with the butt of his gun. That's how I'd found him, lying on the floor. I hadn't known if he was dead or alive. It was terrifying.

He shrugged. "It's a concussion. I'll be fine in a few weeks."

"Will you be able to finish the football season?" I'd watched him play. He was incredibly talented, and just from the pictures in his room, I knew football was his world. I got it. Diving was the same for me.

"I'll be back for the last quarter, if not sooner. It's a mild injury, and I could drive here without a problem."

"I'm surprised your dad let you go. Or that your brother didn't chauffeur you."

He grinned, and I sucked in a breath. God, he was gorgeous. I don't think I would ever get used to that.

"They tried."

I snorted. "I can picture it." He shoved his hands into his pockets, and I admired his athletic form, the broad shoulders, the washboard abs that I knew were beneath this T-shirt—I'd run my hands over them more than once—and how his chest tapered in that sexy *v* to his narrow hips. "Will missing so many games impact next year?"

"It could." He pulled his hands from his pockets and ran them through his hair. "I'll send the coach an email. I should retain my scholarship, but I have no idea about a starting position. That's okay, though. I need to prove myself and earn it."

"You'll have a spot. You're the MVP, right?" My lips twitched because I remembered deciding that MVP, in his case, stood for Most Valuable Prick.

He closed the distance between us and took my hand in his.

Warmth spread through me. "We agreed on a truce while suspended."

I nodded. "Where are you going with this?" I wasn't ready to go back to hating him.

"I don't want to go back to pushing you away. I'm sorry for how I've acted since you got here."

I bit my bottom lip then released it. "I didn't know how your mom died. I get it. I probably would have been worse if the situation was reversed."

That sexy crooked grin curved his lips, and I melted. "And Eliana. I should never have let her in the house."

Her name sucker punched me. "Did you sleep with her?"

He shook his head. "No. I haven't been with anyone since the first time we were together."

Me either. But he already knew that there was no point in admitting the obvious. "So…"

"Things are good between us. Let's keep it that way." He released my hand. "Are you going to dive?"

"Yeah."

"Okay." He turned toward the trail. "I'll meet you at the beach below."

I stayed where I was, watching him until he disappeared. Cole made me feel lighter than I had in a long time. We weren't dating, but we were… something. And I liked it—a lot.

I toed the edge again, working to push our conversation and every other heavy thing on my shoulders from my mind. Picturing the complicated twists and turns I wanted to do, I tensed to push off the edge just as my phone rang. I released the images and stepped back immediately. My heart thundered against my chest, and I scrambled for my phone among my discarded clothes, expecting to see Mom's number. But it wasn't.

It's him.

CHAPTER TWENTY-THREE

COLE

I'm not worried, or so I tried to convince myself as I stood on the beach below where Riley toed the edge of the ledge from an insanely high point on the cliff. She could pull the dive off flawlessly, so I wasn't too concerned about that.

It was her state of mind that bothered me more than anything.

She looked so tiny up there, and I held my breath without meaning to. Just when I thought she would jump, she stepped back. When she reappeared, her phone was in her hand. My vision tunneled. Her stricken expression said everything. I didn't think. I took off at a sprint up the trail.

When I got to the top, Riley already had her clothes in her arms as she ran to meet me. "We have to go."

"Who was that?" I took point on the trail in case someone waited for us at the bottom.

"Nick."

Her strained voice gave me the impression she was barely holding it together. "What the fuck is he doing, calling you?" I was both furious and unsettled about him contacting her.

"I don't know. I hung up as soon as I heard his voice."

We got to the bottom, and she ran to her car. "We should stay together." I met her wide eyes and saw relief at my suggestion.

"Yeah, you're right." Her phone started ringing, and she tossed her clothes into her Charger and the keys at me. "You drive."

She accepted the call and put it on speaker as I slid behind the wheel. The engine roared as her mom's frantic voice filled the interior.

I drove, listening with growing panic.

"Nick's out, Riley."

"I know." Her response was too calm, and I spared her a glance before refocusing on the road. "He called me."

"Oh, God." Raelyn wailed.

"I hung up immediately. Cole is in my car, and we're on our way."

"Good. Good." I could picture her pacing. Dad murmured something unintelligible in the background. "Lucas called in more security, and Ronan is on his way with backup. I don't think he'll get here in time. I told him we'd already be gone. How far are you?"

"We'll be there soon. Try not to worry too much."

A sob sounded at the other end. "I love you, Riles. Please hurry."

"I love you too, Mom." Riley disconnected but kept her phone in a death grip in her lap. "I should have killed him last night."

I agreed. *If the cops hadn't been there...* But they had been, and I couldn't let her go to jail. The statement hung heavily between us, and I didn't say anything because every person in the city seemed to be on the road. Traffic was crazy on a Friday morning. *Shouldn't everyone be at work or school?* I wove in and out of cars when I could, but it was slow going.

The streets were chaos, but inside, the car was eerily silent.

Riley was too calm, too quiet. I wanted to fix everything for her because somehow my feelings for her had gone from hate to want to need. I needed her in my life. That was unsettling.

There wasn't time to analyze any of that as I pulled into the driveway. Men were standing guard by the gate and at the door, and I even saw some patrolling the grounds. Good. I was glad Dad had called in reinforcements. We rushed out of the car and toward the house.

The front door jerked open, and Raelyn ran out, gripped Riley, and hauled her inside. I followed close behind, and Raelyn released Riley long enough to slam the door and lock it. Dad was on the phone a few feet away, barking orders at someone.

"This was a mistake." Raelyn choked back a sob. "I'm sorry. You told me it wouldn't work, and I was selfish. You were right." She tugged Riley farther through the foyer and to the bottom of the stairs. "Go pack. We'll leave as soon as you're ready."

"Raelyn, no." Dad disconnected, intercepting her as Riley started up the stairs. "This is the safest place for you both. I have enough armed guards here to start a war."

She shook her head, and fresh tears trailed over prior streaks. "It was a mistake to involve you and your family. He'll kill you all. I could never live with myself if that happened. I love you, Lucas, but never at the cost of your life or your sons'. This is for the best."

"The hell it is," Dad growled. "I can't lose you again, Raelyn. I'll protect you."

Riley paused on the stairs, and our eyes caught and held.

"You should stay. We'll keep you safe." Dad's head whipped around, and when our gazes collided, it was the first time I'd felt aligned with him, like we were on the same team.

"Where's Damon?" It wasn't his fight, and I didn't want him involved.

"I made him go to school, and then there's the game tonight. There are guards there too."

I nodded, remembering it was Friday. Good. Damon would be safe and ultimately in the dark until it was over. For once, Dad and I were on the same page.

"No." Strength rippled through Raelyn's denial. "He won't come right away because he knows we'll expect that. But we can't stay in the house and wait for him because he will come for us, and you both will be collateral damage. I can't let that happen." She turned to Riley. "Go pack. We're leaving."

Riley nodded then raced up the stairs. Dad tried to reason with Raelyn as I followed Riley. I stood in her doorway, watching her throw everything she owned into a suitcase and a large box. Her sense of urgency clawed at me, as did my rising panic. "Aren't you tired of running?"

She paused for a second then continued tossing things in. "Mom needs me, and even if I was tired of it, it doesn't matter. We'll never be safe here. And if we're here, neither will all of you."

"My dad can use the law to protect you both."

She snorted, slamming the top of her suitcase down then zipping it. "Yeah, legal papers make great shields from knives and bullets."

I didn't move from the doorway, wanting to block her exit. "You know I can fight. Your dad won't get lucky twice."

Riley dropped an armful of clothes from the closet into the box and came to stand before me. For a moment, the panic melted away, and she rested her hand on my chest. "It isn't about Mom and me. It's about you and Damon and your dad, all the people Mom and I care about. I've been doing this my whole life." A sad, accepting smile curved her lips. "It has to be this way."

"I'll come with you." I couldn't let her go, not when I'd come to terms with my feelings. Because I suddenly understood what my dad had been through with Raelyn, at least some of it—his fear of never finding her again if she left. And

I couldn't have that happen with Riley. She was the one for me.

Her head jerked back, and her eyes widened. "You can't, and we both know it. You have school and your whole life here."

"You have me. It should be enough for you to stay."

She shook her head. "You know that's why I have to go." She grabbed her suitcase, leaving the box.

I couldn't bring myself to pick it up. That would have finalized it. I followed her down the stairs. Raelyn was nowhere in sight, and my dad was pacing, his phone pressed against his ear.

Riley opened the door and dragged her suitcase outside, and I rounded on my dad. "Do something."

He hung up and got in my face. "What do you think I'm doing? I've got things in motion and people ready. We'll nail this sick fuck and put him away so he never sees the light of day again."

"Good." I clenched my teeth, barely getting the words out. "And when this is over, you'll come clean to Damon and me about Raelyn, Mom, and anything else you've been keeping to yourself."

Dad gave a clipped nod as Raelyn rushed into the foyer, her suitcase trailing behind. Like lightning, she was outside before Dad could stop her, and not a second later, she popped her head back in. "Tell Riley it's time to go."

Ice infused my veins at what her words could mean. "She's already out there."

"No." Raelyn shook her head. "She's not. Her car's there, and the trunk is open. I saw her suitcase. But she must have gone back in to get the rest."

Fuck. I rushed around Raelyn and to where Riley's car was. She wasn't anywhere. When I rounded the corner to the garage, my heart almost stopped. "Dad!" Two men lay on the grass with their throats slit.

She's gone.

CHAPTER TWENTY-FOUR

RILEY

Pain both dull and sharp throbbed through my skull, and the musty smell didn't help. The surface beneath me was soft like a bed. With effort, I cracked open my eyes and had to blink several times to get my vision to work. Finally, I made out the room's shape—or at least heavy blinds, like the kind in motel rooms, pulled closed.

I'd seen enough of those to know that was where I was. I wracked my brain, trying to remember. *Is Mom here? No...* The last thing I remembered was putting my suitcase in the trunk of my car then blinding pain. I hadn't seen anything but felt the hit. Everything after that was blank.

Only one person could have been behind it: my fucking father.

I felt woozy. Nausea churned my stomach, and I swallowed excess saliva, trying not to throw up as my eyes adjusted even more. My arm was handcuffed to part of the headboard, and I lay on an ugly mustard-colored bedspread with orange and yellow flowers. I pushed myself up, sitting with my back to the headboard.

I scanned the room, ensuring he'd only gotten to me and not

Mom—if he had her, she would be in worse shape than the last time. *Where the hell is Uncle Ronan?*

The metal cuffs rattled as I moved, but I had to check for my phone. My pockets were empty. All I could hope was that the tracking app still worked or had pointed help in the right direction before he disabled and tossed it.

And my shoes were gone. Uncle Ronan had taught Mom and me many things, including the need to keep a long pin tucked inside the material of one of each pair of our shoes. That way, we could pick a lock if needed. It would have come in handy with the stupid handcuffs.

No one was in the room with me, a small saving grace for the time being. Nick had to have been close by with his goons. Suddenly, the door opened, and bright light pierced my brain like a dagger through an eye.

I reeled, trying to stop the tidal wave of nausea brought on by the pain. I got it under control by breathing in through my nose and out through my mouth. I felt him looming near the door. When I managed to open my eyes, he was right where I thought he would be. Close to six feet and broad-shouldered, he leaned against the door, wearing a stupid smirk on his shadowed face. I couldn't make out all his features, but I remembered the dark slicked-back hair from our other unfortunate encounter at Cole's.

"I wasn't sure you were going to wake up. Thought I'd hit you a little too hard."

"Why? What day is it?" My stomach sank. *How far are we from Mom?*

"Sunday."

Have I been out for two days? His smoker's voice grated on my last nerve. "What the hell do you want with me?" I spat venomously. *If only I could kill him just by speaking.*

Silence settled between us. He didn't answer my question, and I refused to repeat myself. Something landed at my side, and I looked down. He'd thrown a bottle of water at me. *Guess he doesn't want me to die... yet.*

I waited for his next move as we stared each other down and he obviously cataloged everything about me. I did the same, as much as my double vision would allow. The asshole had given me a concussion. I hadn't felt the back of my head, but I was sure there was dried blood there.

"You look just like that bitch Raelyn at seventeen."

I bared my teeth at him. *Asshole.*

"As for what I'm going to do with you..." An evil grin curved his mouth, and I barely stopped the bile climbing my throat. Whatever he planned would be some next-level shit. "The contracts are signed. You're going to get me what I want by marrying one of my rivals. We leave in fifteen minutes." He walked out.

"The hell I will!"

He was already gone, but I was sure he'd heard me. I counted back from ten to one, needing to regain control. There wasn't much time to figure out how to get out of there. If I didn't, he would take me back to New York and the hellish future he'd had planned for me, which was too similar to what Mom had escaped. I wasn't having any part of that.

I grabbed the water bottle's cap then heard the satisfying break of the seal, happy that no one had tampered with it. I downed the entire thing, knowing I was dehydrated. Then I twisted to look at what he'd handcuffed me to. With a hard yank, I tested its strength. Nothing. It didn't even budge. The bedpost was solid, but I couldn't figure why, since it was clearly a cheap motel.

And why here? Mom had alluded to him having money. If he was in a big-deal crime syndicate, it was a weird move on his part. Or maybe that was why—Mom would expect him to be at an expensive hotel or traveling to the airport in one of his fancy cars.

Will I ever see her again? And Cole? My heart hurt. Desperation clawed at my throat, and tears filled my eyes. *Fuck it. I can do this.*

I'd watched people dislocate their thumbs in movies, and Uncle Ronan had shown me how to get out of handcuffs that way. He'd taught me a lot of survival skills.

This is going to suck. I turned my head to the side, bit down on a section of my shirt, grabbed my thumb, positioned my knee for added leverage, and then yanked.

Fuck, fuckity, fuck! I panted through the pain. Not wasting too much time, I pulled my hand through the cuff, grabbed the water, and slid off the bed. I wasn't sure how to get my thumb back in, so I left it out of the joint. Hurt like hell, but I would do whatever it took to get out of there.

Once on my feet, I crept unsteadily to the draped windows. Moving the edge of the heavy curtains back a hair to see if the coast was clear, I braced against the pain from the light. It wasn't too bad.

There were two overly large thugs near the window. I eased the curtain back into place then scanned the room again for vents or any other way out. I had no idea where I was or if anyone was coming for me. All I knew from when he'd opened the door was that we were somewhere near the ocean.

CHAPTER TWENTY-FIVE

COLE

It'd been two fucking days with no sighting of Riley or her kidnapper.

Cops were crawling over the woods and all airport, train, and bus stations. And there were too damn many of them downstairs. But they had nothing so far. She had just disappeared, and they weren't doing enough to find her.

I hadn't slept more than a couple of hours. Dad and Raelyn looked like they'd gotten a similar amount of rest—her eyes were red and swollen, and he had dark circles under his. When I'd gone downstairs to see if there was any news, she'd swayed on her feet. Dad was by her side when he wasn't on the phone or working on his contacts. He was completely different around her than he'd been with Mom. I'd noticed it, and so had my brother and cousins.

I didn't even care anymore, though. All that mattered was finding Riley. My chest hurt, and all I could think of was that note I'd found in her room from Nick. I didn't know why she'd kept it—maybe to remind herself that he was a threat so she didn't create a fantasy of him that differed from the reality: he was a dangerous asshole.

I also worried about something I'd overheard Raelyn say to my dad about her brother. She hadn't been able to reach him and thought Nick might have done something to him. When Dad suggested telling the cops, she freaked out. They were at a standstill.

That was how it was with everything, and I couldn't stand it much longer. I barged into Damon's room, and he blinked one eye open. It was eleven, but he'd slept in since it was Sunday and there was no football practice.

I wasn't about to leave Riley's life in the hands of Nick and other people who didn't care about her. The detective had nothing, my dad's contacts had very little, and Raelyn was going just as crazy as I was.

"What are you doing?" Damon asked, his voice rough from sleep.

I yanked open his closet and rummaged around on the top shelf. "Looking for that drone you got for Christmas a year ago."

"Hold up a minute."

When I couldn't find it, I went back into his room and paced. I couldn't sit around and wait any longer.

Damon sat up, and the sheet bunched around his waist.

"I can't sit around and do nothing."

He sighed then ran a hand through his hair. "I get it, but running off without a plan won't help. And you need to clue me in on what's going on. One minute, you want her out. Then she's cool. Then she's not again. Things changed again after her dad broke into the house… so spill."

Fuck, he was right. "We slept together."

"So, your dick is speaking for you?" He snorted.

I took two steps forward then slapped the back of the head. "It's not like that. Well, at first, it kinda was, but then I realized the only thing I hated about her was what our parents and Raelyn had done. Their drama."

"And wanting to make Dad pay. I was down with that too."

"Obviously." We shared a dark look. I still wasn't okay with Dad, and we would need a come-to-Jesus moment when he told all. "At first, it was about payback. But then she got under my skin. Deep. And… I can't imagine being without her. She's fierce and talented. Plus, the loyalty between her and Raelyn is similar to how the four of us are." I sat on the edge of the bed, realizing how deeply I cared. "I love her. She's the one. I feel it in my bones."

He tossed a pillow at me. "I told you she was cool a while back, but you were still on your run-her-out-of-town mission."

I grinned. "Yeah, you did." We fell silent for a few seconds. "So the drone?"

"Oh yeah. It's on the floor in the back-left corner of my closet."

His room was a mess. I had no idea how he found anything in there. "Thanks."

"I don't think the drone will help," he said quietly.

I didn't, either, but if I didn't do something soon, I would go crazy. "What else am I supposed to do?"

"We can listen in on what the cops are saying."

"That's the problem. They're not saying much of anything. And they let him go. Her dad is connected."

"So is ours."

He wasn't kidding. Dad had ties to a ton of influential people. "But nothing's being done. It's been two days. Shit." I went to my room and grabbed the letter I'd swiped from behind her picture. I tossed it on his bed. "Check this out."

I knew the note backward and forward. There wasn't much to it.

You stole from me, Rachel, and I will get her back. I found you once. I'll find you again.

You fucking owe me.

"Raelyn got a text from him that said something about it

almost being Riley's eighteenth birthday," I said. "There's some significance, but I don't know what."

"That's weird. At eighteen, he wouldn't have any rights to her, not that he does anyway. Were they married?"

"I have no idea. Raelyn's engaged to Dad, so I would think not. Unless it's under Rachel whatever her last name is. Then maybe?"

"I hate to say this, but we need to talk to Dad first. They might have more info."

I agreed. "Or he's holding out on us."

It was time for Dad to come clean.

CHAPTER TWENTY-SIX

RILEY

The ticking clock thundered in my ears. I had a window of about fifteen minutes. Dislocating my thumb and breaking out of the handcuffs had taken five.

My body felt weak, shaky, and low on energy. I'd been out cold for two days. The hit on my head couldn't have been the only thing keeping me under. The weird taste in my mouth told me he'd used something else to help with my compliance.

I searched the room as quickly as I could. There wasn't much: side table, bed, TV, and dresser. Nothing of use in the bathroom. I could take a drawer out and hit one of the men with it, but I doubted that would do me any good.

Someone laughed, and I paused then pressed my ear to the dingy wall to hear the unmistakable drone of a TV noise. That was when it clicked. I knew how to escape if I could work quickly enough. I opened the small closet. *Score!* There was a metal rod and three wooden coat hangers. Careful of my thumb, I yanked on the rod until it came loose. *Way to pick the place, Nick.* The cheap motel was perfect for escape. If he'd taken us to a high-end hotel, I doubted I would be able to find a way out, at least not easily.

Still, nothing about what I was about to do would be easy.

Please don't hear me. I tucked the rod under my arm for added support, avoiding my damaged thumb. I gripped it with my uninjured hand then rammed it into the drywall. Sweat beaded along my hairline. The thud echoed like a sonic boom in my ears. I had no idea if it was that loud outside the room.

As soon as I'd made a big enough hole, I set the rod down in the corner of the small closet then tore off pieces of drywall. There wasn't insulation or anything between the studs—I could see the back of the other room's wall. It would have been easier with shoes, but I kicked hard enough to knock out a hole on the other side. It didn't take long to make it big enough. Before I climbed through, I closed the closet door. They would probably look right away, but it could buy me some time.

One leg at a time, I squeezed myself through the hole I'd made. With a cautious push, I opened the door to the new room. After scanning the space, I sighed. It was empty. I still had to get out, though. I rushed to the closed drapes and peeked through a small crack, careful not to move the material too much. I could see the thugs smoking by one of the black sedans, far enough away that I could sneak out and take cover in the parking lot. There were a few cars I could use as a buffer if I crouched and stayed below their line of sight. It was a risk, but waiting was a terrible idea. Too bad the room hadn't been occupied but empty. I would have been able to steal clothes as a disguise. As it was, I was wearing just shorts and a T-shirt.

I unlocked the door, eased it open, and carefully slipped through when a noise sounded at the other end of the sidewalk. *Please don't let that be Nick.* I took a few quick steps behind the side of the closest car and out of sight. No alarm sounded—no pounding footsteps.

Without looking back, I pushed forward, clearing each car until I was at the last one. Then I looked. A jolt of pure fear hit me. Nick was with his goons, heading into the room he'd locked me in. As soon as the door shut, I took off behind the motel. We were close to some woods, and I sprinted as quickly as I could go with a head wound.

Pain radiated through the bottom of my feet from running full out on rocks, sticks, and who knew what else. I put everything I had into making it to the tree line. The first shout pierced the air just as I darted beyond the line of pines. Without looking back, I kept going. I had to put enough distance between us and then hide, hoping they wouldn't find me.

If only I had my phone.

A gunshot boomed, and my heart about stopped. I didn't feel anything, but that didn't mean I hadn't been hit. I kept going deeper into the forest, running on an incline and darting around trees. We were at the base of a mountain. Water roared to my left. I veered that way, hoping the sound would hide the noise I was making.

After another few minutes, I stopped and leaned against a tree to catch my breath. My head pounded like a drum, and my stomach rolled. I gagged but didn't throw up. I was thankful—I needed that water to stay down.

Another shot rang out, but it sounded farther away. My body shook. I had no idea what time it was, only that the sun was going down, and I didn't think anyone would find me in time. I hobbled forward, the pain in my feet acute after the adrenaline rush.

Two days had passed, and no one had found me yet. It was hard to stay positive. Blood coated my left sock, and I'm sure the blood provided an easy trail. I had to find somewhere to hide long enough to figure out what to do. Little black dots crowded the edge of my vision. *Don't pass out.* I inched forward bit by bit, searching as I swayed. I spotted a couple of fallen trees with one crossing the other and almost cried in relief. They butted up to an incline in the mountain, and upon closer inspection, I realized I could crawl behind them and hide. It would be impossible to find me unless they found the exact spot and looked at the small opening in the back.

I squeezed myself behind the trees then contorted my body into a ball. I would sleep for a few minutes then try to find a road and help. I didn't know exactly what Nick had planned, but I knew it involved me marrying some creep and something to do with my mom. He'd been trying to hurt her since she left him. And if he caught her again, I didn't know if she would survive.

CHAPTER TWENTY-SEVEN

COLE

The cops found her phone. It was something, but I wasn't sure if we would get to her in time. Raelyn was like a caged animal. Dad had called a meeting, and I didn't think he'd expected everyone to show, but Shane and Phoenix waded into the deepest trenches with us.

Raelyn sat on one of the chairs in Dad's office, her leg bouncing and her eyes darting from corner to corner. He watched her warily as the four of us filed in. Damon shut the door behind us.

The detective and police were out looking for Riley rather than taking up space inside our house. It was about damn time. Nobody'd had a solid night's sleep since she'd been taken, so two in the morning seemed as appropriate as any other time for us to convene and strategize. Aunt Cece had a shift in the ER but promised to call if there was any news or if a Jane Doe fitting Riley's description came in.

"Where was her phone?" I wanted details.

"Along one of the mountain passes," Dad said. "Nick shut it off and popped the battery before tossing it out of the car. They found her shoes a few feet from it."

"She can't make a run for it?" Shane asked.

"That, and in case something was hidden in them." Raelyn grabbed the arms of the chair, digging her nails into them. "If he cuffs her, she doesn't have anything on her to pick the lock or shoelaces to help break a zip tie."

Damon's head snapped back. "Whoa, she was prepared for that?"

"Nick Viareggio is Mafia." Dad rested his elbows on his desk, his phone in front of him. "Raelyn's brother prepared both of them for what would happen if Nick found them."

I turned to Raelyn. "Where is your brother when she needs him the most?" I couldn't keep the anger from my voice.

"He should already be here." A tear slid down her face, and she shook her head. "The only thing that would keep him away is if Nick got to him first."

"What is Nick to you, Raelyn?" I kept my voice low to mask the barely contained violence thrumming through me. "Husband? Lover?"

She pressed her lips into a tight line, leaching all the color from them, and seemed to gather herself for a moment. "He was a mistake. I snuck out of my very religious parents' house to go to a party with some friends. I was barely sixteen. I knew my older brother, who was supposed to keep an eye on me, wouldn't be there and thought I could get away with it." She waved her hand as if to speed up the memory. "I drank too much, and Nick was watching me, filling my cup when it was empty. We weren't anything. He'd shown interest in me, but my brother, Ronan, was very protective and warned him to stay away from me.

"Ronan wasn't there that night, and I wasn't thinking right. A few months later, I found out that I was pregnant. And when my parents learned about my condition, they went to a meeting with Nick and his father. I guess Nick wanted more with me. I was to marry him a few weeks after they all met. There was a contract because he was Mafia, and they compensated my parents."

"That's fucked up." I glanced at Dad, but he didn't seem shocked. *He knew? He must have.* "Did you go through with the wedding?"

She jerked her head in a nod. "I didn't have a choice." Her voice was barely a whisper. "Two weeks after, I escaped."

"So he's your husband?" Damon asked.

She shrugged and glanced at my dad, but he was calm and clearly in the know. She met Damon's eyes but then looked away. "Yes and no. Ronan is five years older than me and was already heavily entrenched in a rival syndicate. I went to my brother with the news, and he helped me when I was able to escape by hiding me in an apartment rented under an alias. I had Riley there, not in a hospital, with the help of a nurse Ronan knew. Nick learned that I'd miscarried through false information fed to him."

"And your parents? Did they help you?" Phoenix asked.

"No." Steel infused her voice. "And I never asked about them after I ran away. One day, when Ronan was visiting and playing with Riley, who was a few months old, I went out for a walk." Her face softened. "I met your dad. The rest of the story, you know." She shuddered. "Nick found me and beat me so badly that I almost died. Ronan and some of his guys found me in time. Then a few days later, he staged my death. They filed a death certificate and held a small service. So although I married him, it was complicated. Because who I was back then is dead."

"But he found out you were alive?" It was crazy. I never could have made it up even in my wildest nightmares.

"Yes. An acquaintance of his saw me and relayed the news to him. Nick... didn't learn that Riley was alive until she was thirteen. He's been searching for us more intensely even than when he thought it was just me."

I had no words. Her story was a nightmare. But something

else bothered me, and I shifted my focus to Dad. "And you? Weren't you already married to Mom? I would have been a few months older than Riley then."

He grimaced, and I knew I wouldn't like what he had to say.

"I don't want you to think badly of your mom. She loved you both, so remember that."

I had no doubt about her feelings toward Damon and me.

"Linda and I never dated in college. Her sister"—he notched his head in Phoenix and Shane's direction, indicating their mom, Aunt Cece—"was dating Joe Wrenshall"—our cousins' dad. "Linda and I were together one night after a party. I'd just found out I was invited to the draft, and we celebrated hard."

It was the first time Dad had mentioned the NFL draft. Damon and I'd heard about it from Mom on the weekend she killed herself.

"When Linda told me she was pregnant, I had some things to consider seriously. She and I always struggled, having barely known one another before we married, but that first year and a half were hardest for me. What probably made the situation worse was that I questioned everything, whether I'd made the right choice by passing on the NFL, going for my law degree, then opening the firm. Then I met Raelyn… and knew instantly that she was the one for me." He shrugged. "I don't know how to explain it. I've just always known."

I shifted uncomfortably in my seat. Because I did know. Riley had the same effect on me. It helped a little to understand the chaos that had always existed in our family and why.

"But your mother… I couldn't leave her. She wasn't always… stable."

Silence fell. Things finally made sense, and I could put it to bed. "And Nick? Does he have any legal claim to her?"

Raelyn shook her head, but Dad was the one to answer. "No. I've filed so many charges against him that he'll live out the rest of his days in a prison cell. There's no legal proof she's his daughter."

He'd been charged with attacking Riley and me, breaking and entering, and who knew what else Dad had thrown on top of that. But his lawyers, bribes, or both had gotten him out once. It worried me that he could do it again.

"Is there any other news?" Phoenix leaned forward, elbows to knees, and got us back on track. "We should go search for her too."

As soon as Dad gave us the location and any other details, I was there.

"She's out there somewhere. He'll want her alive." Raelyn trembled, and her face took on a pale-greenish shade. "She's property in his mind, and he plans to use her to further his power in the syndicate."

"What the hell does that mean?" I lurched to my feet, not liking the direction of this new twist one bit.

"That he'll marry her"—she swallowed audibly, her voice shaking—"to whoever will give him the most in return."

It was a gut punch. "Who does that in this day and age?" I felt powerless. "We need to get to her. I'm tired of sitting around and doing nothing." I swung my gaze to Dad. "Where was her phone found? We can start looking there."

"There's more." Dad glanced at Raelyn. "Shots were fired at a motel. They investigated, and the reports match Nick's description."

Raelyn's phone rang, and she tapped it then whipped it to her ear. "Ronan?" It came out as more of a cry. "Are you okay?"

Dad stood and went to her, gently taking the phone and hitting the speaker button. "Lucas Savage here. Have you found Riley?"

"No, but I know about where she'll be." Ronan rattled off something about some woods behind a motel. He said she would've gone deep into the woods and, once it was safe, tried to find a road.

"We're coming." Raelyn sounded invigorated as she rushed out the door.

Dad finished the call, and we all raced after her. I exchanged a look with my brother and cousins. I didn't need to say anything. They were with me. Damon and I piled into his SUV, and Phoenix and Shane took one of theirs. Then we were off, not far behind Dad and Raelyn.

If I'd had questions about my feelings for Riley before, I had zero doubts left. She was it. I just worried I might be too late, and she would forcefully be given to another.

CHAPTER TWENTY-EIGHT

RILEY

Everything hurt. I stifled a groan. I couldn't make a sound. Not yet. Not until I was sure no one was nearby, waiting to capture me or worse.

Cole filled my mind as I huddled there, trying to determine what I should do next. He'd fought to keep Nick away from me when he broke into their home, and I replayed that before turning to how exhilarating fighting with him was—the back-and-forth blackmail had been a thrill. Then there was the way a simple touch from him set my whole body on fire.

He makes me feel safe. He makes me feel.

I'd always kept my emotions under control. But around him, there was no stopping their violent tsunami. And the more I thought about it, I realized I'd always wanted him and that I… *loved* him. The realization shocked me. We'd begun our relationship with hate. But that was gone. I just wanted him.

If I get out of here alive, I'm telling him everything.

The chill during the night had seeped into my bones. I stood still, listening before attempting to move from behind the fallen trees.

A few birds chirped overhead, and something small scurried

through the brush. A rush of air pushed past my numb lips. It was time to move. My head throbbed in tune with my heartbeat, a thundering, steady pulse that echoed behind my eyes. I couldn't feel my feet or hands, which was partly good, given how mangled they were. At least with little feeling, I would be able to walk.

In agonizing increments, I uncurled from the fetal position I'd had to assume to remain hidden. Minutes later, once I'd managed to wiggle my way out from behind the trees and step out from the makeshift hole, I leaned against the bark, more shaken than I would have liked.

Thready beams of sunlight shot diagonally through the canopy of pines above. The angle of the sun said it was early morning. I stayed there, leaning against the downed tree, acclimating to my surroundings and giving my body a moment to get the blood flowing.

I had no idea where I was or how far I needed to go to find a road or someone who could help. The sound of waves was barely perceptible—I had to have been far enough away from a cliff or beach that it made sense to continue moving in the other direction and down. I had to find civilization.

I pushed myself off the log to stand on my own, swaying for the minute it took to gain enough balance to take a step. Sharp jolts of pain shot from my feet and up my legs, settling in my churning, empty stomach.

This sucks. I took another painful step. Alive was better than dead. I kept moving slowly. If the motel was almost directly below where I was on the mountain, I would run into a road if I went that way—I knew one wound up the hillside. Once I found it, I could walk along the edge. And if Nick or his goons appeared in their shiny black Mercedes, I would dive back into the woods for cover, hopefully before they spotted me.

I wasn't sure how much time passed as I staggered across pine-needle-strewn ground, in a mostly straight line through the trees. At one point, I picked up a stick long enough to use as a cane. My hand with the dislocated thumb was swollen and mostly useless—good thing my other one wasn't damaged.

My mind kept wandering. There had been gunshots at the motel. That had to mean cops had been called. *Please let Nick be dead or gravely injured.* That would have solved so many problems. I couldn't let my thoughts go to any other horrifying scenario, like Cole finding me and Nick turning the gun on him.

I gagged, the thought too much to handle. I panted and swayed, unsure how much farther I could go. Something sounded off in the distance. *Is someone calling for me?* A twig snapped, and I blinked back into focus with sheer determination. It had been close. Tightening my grip on the stick, I turned and swung with all my might.

A hoarse yell tore from my throat as the branch made impact with a large form. The strike reverberated from the wood up my hand and then my arm. I stumbled back but steadied myself to hit him again.

"Riley!"

I didn't know where to look. My vision blinked in and out, and whoever screamed my name sounded simultaneously from behind and in front of me. I wobbled. The stick was gone from my hand. *How...?* Black spots multiplied, clouding my vision further. Someone grabbed my arm, and I flung myself back with the last of my strength. I didn't hit the ground but fell into something hard.

Everything whirled out of control until I couldn't fight anymore and the darkness converged and dragged me under.

CHAPTER TWENTY-NINE

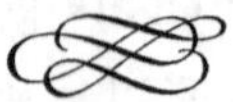

COLE

Riley was close. I could sense her. I whirled when I heard movement.

"Riley!" Ronan grunted, and I caught sight of a branch making contact with the side of his head.

I sprinted, zigzagging through the trees with Phoenix, Damon, and Shane close on my heels. Then I saw a mass of chestnut hair. Dirt and blood. Some fresh, some old. I lunged forward as Ronan reached for her. Confusion and fear clouded her face, and she swatted his hand away, lost her balance, and melted back. I skidded to a stop just as she crumpled into me.

I lifted her with ease, cradling her gently. Ronan growled, crowding me. We'd met only few hours before, after he'd contacted Raelyn with the location where he thought Riley would be. Both he and Dad had argued against her mom coming with us. The only way they could keep her from staying away was by bringing her to the mountain's base and surrounding her with security. Dad stayed because he and Ronan feared she would slip out somehow and get herself taken by Nick's associates. There was something else they weren't saying... I would find out eventually. Secrets rarely stayed buried for long.

Ronan reached for her, but I turned away. "I've got her."

He gripped my shoulder, holding me in place. "Listen, punk. The only reason I'm letting you carry my niece is because you caught her when she was falling." He dug his fingers into me as he leaned close to my ear. "If you hurt her in the slightest, it'll be the last time you see her, and you'll never see me coming."

I glared over my shoulder. "That won't happen. Riley means more to me than anything."

"More than football? Because that's what you'll lose, your ability to play."

"She's incomparable."

Ronan grunted and released my shoulder. Something settled in me, knowing that she also had him in her corner. Ronan, Damon, Phoenix, and Shane surrounded my sides and back, protecting her as we made our way off the mountain.

The blood and slight weight of her filled me with terror. I needed to see her eyes open and have her give me hell about being carried. I could feel the movement of her chest as she drew shallow breaths, and the enormity of my feelings for her almost took me out at the knees. I would go to any length to keep Riley safe. There was nothing I wouldn't do for her. And I knew without a doubt that we would belong to each other one day.

CHAPTER THIRTY

RILEY

Mom eased onto the bed Tuesday night, careful not to jar me. "How are you feeling?"

I'd only been in the hospital for one night—it wasn't as if I'd died. "I'm fine." I tossed the ice pack from my chilled hand to the floor then slipped it under the luxurious white duvet.

She snorted. "Fine is never a good thing." She brushed my hair from my face. "Tell me how you're really doing."

"Everything hurts, but it's temporary." I fought against my eyelids closing. The lighting was dim in my room, tempting me to pass out again. "I'm just tired."

"I get it. Healing is a journey."

If anyone understood going a round in the ring with Nick, it was Mom. I didn't need to sugarcoat or make anything up. It was also just nice to have her in my room, where we could talk. I just wished I wasn't so tired. "Very profound, Mom." I laughed as she rolled her eyes.

"You know why I did what I did with Lucas, right?"

I scooted up so my back was against the headboard, and she shifted to face me. "What? With moving in here? You explained all that… a little late." I scowled at her. "You could have filled me in the first night we moved here."

She pursed her lips. "I could've. But Lucas and I were ironing out a few things between us."

"Marriage? That's what you guys were fighting about in the kitchen when Cole and I walked in."

"It was, but that wasn't the only thing. I'd finally told him everything. About my parents, the Mafia connections, your uncle… None of it mattered to him. He was stubborn, and I was afraid for him—for all of us."

"Then why didn't we leave? I tried to get you to. Nick could've killed them. He came close with Cole."

She shuddered. "I am foolish and very in love. Lucas was so persuasive. He'd hired security that was secretly keeping an eye on everyone."

It was my turn to snort. "Lot of good that did."

"Yeah. I don't think they quite understood the lengths Nick would go to get at both of us."

"Back to the 'in love' part. What did you decide about marrying him?"

Light danced in Mom's eyes, and I had my answer before she uttered a word. "How do you feel about it? Because your opinion means the world to me, Riles."

I wanted to roll my eyes because it hadn't mattered much when I wanted to leave. But I also got it, mostly because of how I felt about Cole. I was so drawn to him that leaving would've felt like cutting off a limb. Mom had loved Lucas from afar for so many years, and I would never deny her any amount of happiness. "I say do it. And on the plus side, no more cons." I winked at her.

A soft smile curved her lips. "It was fun, though. We were damn good at it."

"Of course we were. Look where we come from."

"How do you feel about having Lucas as a stepdad?"

"Weird. He'll always be Cole's dad to me. I won't see him any other way, even after you marry him."

"But you're good with it? Because if you aren't, Riles, I don't have to marry him. You're my life and always come first."

I squeezed her hand. "I'm good with it. Marry the guy and get your happy ever after."

She scooted forward and wrapped me carefully in her arms. The pain wasn't as bad as everyone thought, but Nick taking me had scared ten years off their lives, from what Mom had said. My uncle had just waded in, guns a-blazing. Mom and I were lucky to have him in our lives.

When she released me, something in her expression caused me to brace for whatever was next.

"Cole carried you off the mountain. Cole and not your uncle." She paused, and we both let the significance sink in. It said something that Uncle Ronan had allowed it. "You were cradled in Cole's arms, surrounded by Ronan, Damon, and their cousins. I…" She tried to blink back tears, but they rolled down her cheeks. With a swipe of her hand, she brushed them away then took a deep breath, getting her emotions under control. "The expression on his face… I know how he feels about you. I would have been blind not to see it."

This is the big talk. Mom and I had been strangers, given how little we'd seen of each other while living in the Savage house—manor, mansion, whatever. But I was ready. There was no going back. Cole had defended me against Nick, almost at the cost of his own life. "I think we're dating."

She grabbed my hands. "I should have known there was something between you two by the sparks that flew every time you were in the same room."

"We also kind of hated each other, so I can see how you missed the signals." I grinned then stifled a yawn.

"This is weird because we have such a different relationship than most mothers and daughters."

I wanted to head it off fast. "We do. And I love how we are, so don't try to change it."

Her shoulders went down about two inches, the tension visibly draining from her. "Okay. I can see how tired you are, so I'll let you sleep after this suggestion. Please take things slow. You've had an unconventional upbringing and never got to be a kid like most. Go to college. Have fun. Date other people if you want. Don't lock yourself into a serious relationship with the first guy you fall for."

If only it were that simple. "I'll do most of those things, Mom, but Cole's... different."

She worried her lower lip with her teeth for a moment, and I let her see how sincere I was about my feelings. I meant it. No one had ever made me feel the way he did, and I couldn't imagine anyone ever coming close.

CHAPTER THIRTY-ONE

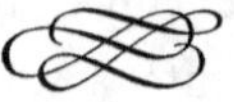

COLE

I'd never been so glad for a concussion. It enabled me to stay home from school and practice. Nothing could keep me from Riley, and my head injury made staying with her easier. No one questioned me.

We'd found her Monday morning, and it was already Wednesday. She'd stayed overnight at the hospital due to doctors having to address her injuries—her own concussion, multiple deep lacerations on her feet, stitches on her head, a reset and splinted thumb, and IV fluids for extreme dehydration. Raelyn and Dad had brought her home on Tuesday. I'd stayed at the hospital, too, but it wasn't the same in the waiting room.

Raelyn hovered, and I had to give them space. But at night, she returned to Dad's room, and that was when I slipped into bed with Riley. Exhausted, she barely stirred when I took her in my arms.

Leaving before first light was the hardest thing I had to do. I didn't think she knew I'd been in there because she was on heavy painkillers. I'd overheard her telling Raelyn she only wanted them last night and to flush the rest, another show of strength that awed me.

Still in recovery mode but not for much longer, I skipped running and did a light lifting session in the home gym. When I came into the kitchen to get some more water, I found Riley at the island, eating yogurt with one foot propped on the stool next to her. She was pale and had dark half-moons hanging beneath her eyes but looked more beautiful than ever.

"Hey." I carefully lifted her foot, sat on the stool next to her, and lowered it onto my lap. "How are you feeling?"

"Like a truck ran me over." She swallowed another spoonful before setting her yogurt aside. "Thank you for searching for me."

"You never have to thank me for coming for you. I'll always be there, no matter what trouble you get yourself into." I winked, trying to lighten the mood a little. She started to smile, but it fell in the next second.

"Did you hear about him?"

I nodded. "Nick's in a coma—"

"From a gunshot wound to the head." She leveled me with a look that said she knew there was more to it. "And they said there isn't any brain activity. He's not going to wake up."

We didn't say who shot him because it had obviously been her uncle. He hadn't come right away—Nick had ambushed him. Once he managed to get a bead on Nick at the motel, he'd shot him and the thugs with him, somehow making it look like an internal shootout. There was no recording at the motel. It'd mysteriously disappeared. No one questioned it because of who Nick was.

Cops were crawling all over the scene, and it took time to learn that they hadn't recovered Riley. Then the search was on, and we all participated.

"We haven't had a chance to talk." I needed to know what had happened—all of it.

"Yeah. But can we go somewhere more comfortable?"

I stood, picked her up, then carried her to the couch. I kept her cradled in my arms, unwilling to sever the connection. Once comfortable, she told me everything: how Nick had hit her over the head from behind, and she'd woken two days later in the motel. How she'd escaped and where she'd hidden. I was so damn proud of her.

"When I hid on the mountain, unsure if I would make it out alive, I promised myself something."

I cupped the back of her neck and traced the curve of her face with my thumb. "What's that?" I dropped my gaze to her lips, needing to kiss her.

"I realized that through all the miniwars we waged between us, I developed feelings for you."

I held still, drowning in her warm brown eyes, afraid to hope that she returned even a fraction of how I felt about her.

"I love you, Cole."

My vision tunneled. All I saw was her. "When we first met, you barreled into my life."

She laughed. "Literally, both times."

I grinned, happier than I'd ever been. "And every step of the way, you challenged me. I think I fell for you from the moment we collided. I love you, too, Riley." Then I kissed her.

EPILOGUE

RILEY

I stood on the beach, back where it all began. Water lapped at my toes. I dug them into the sand, enjoying the kiss of frothy waves against my skin as they rearranged the shore in subtle ways.

A little over a year ago, last summer, I'd crashed a party down the beach, wanting to do something fun without an agenda. I laughed under my breath. Everything had changed once we moved into that house.

Cole had left an indelible impression on me that night. His over-the-top alpha attitude goaded me to push his buttons, and I'd never had more fun. Mom had been right. This town was different. We'd agreed that it was the first place that had felt like home to us.

Uncle Ronan came around every so often and got along with Lucas, which was unexpected. And Mom's relationship with Lucas was solid. They planned to get married in the summer. It was late March, and Lucas had pushed for an immediate wedding, but Mom wanted to wait. She'd said it was enough that they lived together. In private, she told me that waiting was torture, but a lot had happened, and summer would come soon enough. She wanted the boys to be comfortable with the idea rather than rushing ahead.

By that point, I didn't think they would care. Well, Damon might have. He hadn't let go of hating his father. Cole was good, though. They'd had some big discussion when I was running for my life, and it had settled things enough for him to put their differences behind them.

I pulled the blue-and-purple beach towel out of my bag, careful not to launch the letter I had in there into the water. I spread the towel on the sand then sat, extending my legs and crossing them at the ankle. The bag was beside me, and a giddy excitement raced through me.

I'd texted Cole to meet me on the beach behind his house. I wanted to open the letter from Thane together. I glanced at my phone for the hundredth time. He'd texted that he was on his way ten minutes ago. I couldn't wait.

"Hey." He dropped onto the beach towel next to me, having moved as silently as he always did. He leaned in for a kiss and lingered.

When he pulled back and grinned, I couldn't help from touching my lips with my fingertips. "That never gets old."

Cole's deep, throaty laughter sent a jolt of longing through me. I started to lean into him but then remembered why I'd wanted to meet. I twisted around and grabbed the envelope from my bag. "I have news." I sank my teeth into my bottom lip, tapping my foot rapidly, nervous about what the envelope contained.

"From Thane?" Cole's dark brows rose. "You know there's nothing to be nervous about. You have straight As, and the coach already spilled about your scholarship."

"Pending acceptance." I frowned. "You never know... I've gone to a lot of schools... and I mean a *lot*."

He smirked, and I couldn't help but think my uncle was rubbing off on him. "But they don't know that. Your uncle fixed it so it looked like you only went to two high schools, finishing here at Hidden Valley."

Everything he said made sense, but it was still huge. "I never thought I would go away to school. It's always been me and Mom."

"Why? Raelyn's been talking about putting down roots and you going to college since you moved here last summer."

He had a point. "Right. But I didn't believe it. Not until a little while ago." I slid my finger beneath the flap and eased the envelope open. When I withdrew the letter, the first thing I saw was the bold "Congratulations." "I got in!" I didn't bother to read the rest and launched myself into Cole's arms.

He caught me like I knew he would.

When he released me so I could shift around and sit with my back to his chest, I held the letter, and we both read it. Academic and sports scholarships had combined to get me a full ride, including living in the dorm. I would have to pay for books, but that was the only added cost. Toward the bottom, there was a note saying that the athletic department would be contacting me soon with details about the preseason start and move-in dates.

"Have you spoken to your coach?" Thane had recruited Cole hard. He'd mentioned a few conversations and emails. I'd glanced at one he'd left open on his phone one day when he left his room—and me in his bed—to get us something to eat. We'd been hanging out after sex, talking, when an email came through. The coach had guaranteed him a starting position.

"After signing day?"

I laced my fingers with his. That had been an event too. Reporters had been there, along with the university coaches. Lucas was in the pictures, and there had been a small write-up in the paper about his stats and time at Thane. I had no idea it was such a big deal, but I shouldn't have been surprised. Cole was treated like a god by both the community and his peers.

When he went onto the field, the fans thundered in excitement. It was an experience.

"Once, but only to give me move-in details."

Things were moving quickly. "It's going to be weird." A part of me was sad about leaving.

"What's that?"

"Living in different dorms. Sleeping apart." We'd been sneaking to each other's rooms at night since my abduction. Mom knew—I'd confided in her. We were back to being close, and I never wanted that to change. I understood why she'd acted the way she had. Lucas was the love of her life, and she'd been wrapped up in reconnecting as he strategized and applied pressure on others to keep us safe. If Nick had lived, Lucas would have had enough evidence, aside from the abduction, to put him away for life and then some.

As for Cole and us sleeping together... we'd kept that little detail from Lucas as much as possible. He felt responsible for his son corrupting me. It hadn't taken long, thanks to Mom, for him to come around to accepting our relationship—not about sleeping in the same room, just that we were serious.

Cole's arms tightened around me. "You think that's going to happen? You'll be crashing at the football house, or I'll sneak into your dorm room."

"Every night?"

"Count on it, Riles." His pupils dilated, and he briefly dropped his gaze to my lips.

"Cass got into Thane too. We talked about rooming together."

"Better let her know about the sleeping arrangements ahead of time."

I snorted. "I think she'll be in a similar boat. Matt Chambers is going there too. So are a bunch of people from the academy."

"No one else matters but you, my brother, and my cousins."

I wasn't surprised. He didn't pay much attention to people

other than the ones he cared about, and his circle was small: his brother, cousins, and me.

"Screw it. Let's get a place together when we're there. We'll have a year where it's just us before they move in too."

I laughed. He thought if he could keep me all to himself, there wouldn't be any problems. But I could already sense something brewing with Damon, and my mind skipped to the black-haired girl I'd seen him arguing with in the halls—Skylar. I still owed her for being so cool about the school article. Then there were Phoenix and Shane.

Cole was kidding himself. Trouble would find us somehow. *Let it.* I had every confidence based on what Cole and I had already been through. We would weather any storm and come out stronger for it.

"We can wait. It'll be tough but worth it. Besides, Damon and your cousins will be coming our sophomore year, and they have to stay in the football house as freshmen. We can get a place with everyone in our junior year."

"No matter where we live, next year will be the best because I'll have you with me."

I wrapped my arms around him, brushing my lips against his. "Always." Before things got too heavy between us—I could barely restrain myself, and I sensed the same need in him—I said, "Let's get everyone and go to the cove to celebrate."

"Later. I've got you all to myself, and I'm not ready to share your attention." Then he kissed me, and I forgot everything except how his lips felt against mine.

The End

Except from Brutal Days

Our eyes met and held, and I hardened myself to the fireworks exploding inside my body at his nearness.

"I want to make a deal with you." I kept my voice low so no one could overhear what I was about to say. It was one of those spur-of-the-moment things that I had no plan to back up but that escaped my mouth before I could stop it. "I'll do your homework in all your classes for as long as you date Gia."

My heart thundered against my ribcage so hard I thought it would crack. Beads of sweat formed along my hairline. I felt wild and out of control, not my usual self. A sexy, devious smirk slowly tugged at his lips, and I found myself holding my breath.

"I have a counteroffer," he said.

But then the teacher called the class to order. The glimmer in his eye made something tingle in my stomach as we broke apart to take our seats. The scary thing was, I planned to listen to his terms.

Continue reading the Hidden Valley Elite series with Brutal Days:
https://www.islavaughnauthor.com/books

Keep up with Isla's releases by joining her newsletter:
https://bit.ly/IslaVaughnNewsletter
If you enjoyed reading SAVAGE TRUTH as much as I did writing it, I hope you'll consider leaving a review.

ABOUT THE AUTHOR

Isla Vaughn is the author of the Hidden Valley Elite series. Her romance books are full of complex characters, strong alpha males, and the fierce women who bring them to their knees. When not writing, she can be found daydreaming about owning a beach house, reading, or drinking too much coffee.
You can find her at:
https://www.islavaughnauthor.com

Subscribe to Isla's newsletter for cover reveals, book announcements, and giveaways: https://bit.ly/IslaVaughnNewsletter

facebook.com/author.IslaVaughn

instagram.com/islavaughnauthor

goodreads.com/islavaughn_author

bookbub.com/profile/isla-vaughn

tiktok.com/@islavaughnauthor

twitter.com/IVaughn_Author

ALSO BY ISLA VAUGHN

Hidden Valley Elite Series

Savage Start

Savage Lies

Savage Truth

Brutal Days

Brutal Nights

Cruel Start

Cruel Hate

Cruel Love

Wicked Games

Wicked Ends